THE FARMER
TAKES A WIFE

A LAS MORENAS NOVELLA

Genevieve Turner

Book Layout ©2013 BookDesignTemplates.com

The Farmer Takes a Wife/ Genevieve Turner. -- 1st ed.
ISBN 978-1511866095

For S (not aka B)

CHAPTER ONE

San Jacinto Mountains, Spring 1897

TONIGHT WAS THE NIGHT.

Marcus Gries smoothed a hand down his shirtfront to bolster his courage, his clammy palm catching slightly on the starched linen.

He'd left nothing to chance. His best suit was clean and pressed, thanks to Widow Sand. He'd scrubbed every inch of his body in the tub not more than an hour ago, his skin still tight from the soap. He'd slicked his hair flat with perhaps a bit too much pomade—but he wanted to be certain it would stay in place. He'd briefly considered running some pomade through his beard along with a comb but had decided that would be going too far.

He resisted the urge to scratch under his itchy shirt. The stiffness of his skin, suit, and hair were all necessary—a man didn't march off to court his future wife in faded overalls with dirt under his nails. No matter how much more comfortable he might be in those overalls.

Tonight was the night. After two years of waiting for the chance to dance with her, to *speak* with her, he was finally going to approach Miss Laura Kemper. Condi-

1

tions wouldn't be any better than tonight for approaching her; he'd read that as clearly as he could the weather. The Dragon would be gone tonight. He'd heard from Luke Crivelli, who'd heard from his sister, that the Dragon wasn't feeling well and would be staying home. Good enough authority for Marcus to act.

Now all he needed to do was take that first step toward the barn door, the same door with all the light, music, and laughter spilling out of it. He leaned forward, waiting for legs to begin to carry him...

His legs refused to move.

Drat his weak, silly nerves. He took a shaky breath, then closed his eyes, the better to call up Miss Kemper's sweet face. And the light in church as it caught on her hair, the same color as fresh straw. Then her slate-blue eyes as they stared into his from across the counter at her brother's mercantile. Finally, her warm smile greeting him as they passed on the streets of Cabrillo.

He opened his eyes, released a breath. Oh yes, that was better. He patted his stomach, calm once more, touched a fingertip to the edge of his mouth, which had tipped up at the memory of Miss Kemper's, and shook out his legs, which had finally decided to obey him.

He leaned forward once more and commanded his feet to *move*. He lurched ahead, stumbling past the open door and into the warm gaiety within. He stopped at the edge of the crowd, for once pleased to be a full head higher than most of the men here. He let his gaze dash over everyone's heads, looking for that particular glint of gold embossed in his memory.

There. There it was, in the far corner of the barn. His heart broke into a lope, and his cheeks heated. *Miss Kemper*. He was truly going to do this.

He couldn't see her face from here but knew it was her from her movements. He had never seen a lady with such quiet, natural grace. She moved the same way birds soared, effortlessly and without a sound. If she agreed to dance with him, she'd move just as gracefully in his arms. His legs got shaky at that thought, so he shoved it away and pushed himself through the crowd.

"Marcus!" Mr. Whitman thundered, clasping his hand. "How are you?"

Marcus shook just long enough to be polite. "Well. And how are you?" He craned his neck, keeping that glint of gold within his sight.

"Fine, fine."

Before the second "fine" was out of Mr. Whitman's mouth, Marcus was moving on. He couldn't stop now lest his bravado desert him.

It was tonight or never.

"Hello, Marcus."

He paused for half a moment at the chorus of female voices. "Miss Agnes, Miss Franny."

They giggled together, all of sixteen and giddy with it. "Where are you headed, dressed like you are?"

He grinned back at her—he liked Miss Franny. "Wouldn't you like to know?"

And he kept on moving toward that glint of gold. After all, he had an important commission tonight.

When he was within a few feet of her, the crowd parted and his chest tightened. She was turned away, her face hidden, but the light tangled in the curls pinned at her nape in a way that made his gut ache. Her dress was a pearly gray that suited her well, clinging to the fine lines of her figure in a neither quiet nor showy manner. Like Miss Kemper, it announced itself with a dignity that need not shout.

And now he had to go speak with her. The air caught in his lungs.

No. No, he'd waited too long for this. His nerve would not fail him.

He released a sigh and moved forward, reaching out to touch her arm to catch her attention. His heart thundered, his mouth going dry. He was truly going to do it—

His heart shuddered, all of him seizing.

The Dragon was not at home.

No, the Dragon was right here, standing next to Miss Kemper—and staring at Marcus. His entire length went clammy and shaky.

His legs began to take him backward before either of them noticed him.

Too late. The Dragon smiled wide, revealing a row of pearly teeth. "Why, Mr. Gries," Miss Moreno trilled.

Most men upon seeing Miss Catarina Moreno wouldn't call her a dragon. They'd likely say she was the most beautiful woman they'd ever seen. Or they'd say she resembled something beautifully exotic, like a tiger.

But to Marcus she was a dragon. Not one of those dragons that stomped through forests, fighting knights in armor. Rather a Chinese dragon, like the ones in the pictures the citrus pickers had.

The sinuous Miss Moreno *could* breathe fire, but was much more likely to scramble up a man's pant leg and bite his privates.

But Miss Kemper was no dragon. If he had to describe her, he'd say she was like a quail, a bird that spent most of its time hidden in the brush. Once you'd seen it, however, you kept longing for one more glimpse.

He could look at Miss Kemper all day.

Miss Moreno was part of the reason he hadn't approached Miss Kemper, since no matter where they were, Miss Moreno was always by Miss Kemper's side, surrounded by adoring suitors and making clever but cutting remarks about farmers and dirt whenever he got near.

Being the only farmer in an area full of cattlemen, he was used to his fair share of ribbing. But when Miss Kemper smiled at Miss Moreno's remarks—it cut him to the quick.

It didn't help that every time he caught sight of Miss Kemper, with her soft eyes and gentle smile, his heart sped up double time while his faculties slowed to a standstill. He might squeeze out a *hello* or *how are you* if he was lucky, but not much more.

Tonight was to have been the night, the moment when he dared all for her without braving the sneers of Miss Moreno. And now it was all ruined. He could turn tail, run back to his farm—heck, run all the way down the mountain to his family's farm in the valley.

But then Miss Kemper turned to him, a smile warming her expression, her soft blue gaze rooting him in place. All of him slowed, stilled, as her attention came fully to him.

This. This was what he'd come here for tonight, her welcoming smile and happy expression. She looked as if she wanted to hear his voice. As if that was what she'd been waiting for.

Come on, tongue. Don't fail me now.

"How are your potatoes, Mr. Gries?" More of a dart than a question, but that was usual for Miss Moreno. The men clustered around her sniggered.

He didn't even give her the courtesy of a glance—not that he could have looked away from Miss Kemper. "Quite well, Miss Moreno. And how are yours?"

Miss Kemper looked right back, that soft smile never fading. His heart beat strongly, surely, with no nervous skitters. He could do this.

"Mine are doing well, but I'm not trying to irrigate forty acres—"

"Miss Kemper?" He reached out his hand, ignoring the Dragon's fiery sputters. "Would you care to dance with me?"

Her smile went cold and stiff for half a moment, and his heart dove for the floor. She was going to say no. He'd risked asking her and—

A wider, warmer smile stretched her mouth. "I would love to, Mr. Gries."

Then, wonder of wonders, she put that soft hand into his.

She'd said yes. *He was holding her hand.*

If his nerves were shaky before, they were downright quivering now as her delicate skin pressed against his. He pressed back, but gently, gently—his calluses must not harm her. *Settle down*, he warned his nerves. He couldn't properly dance if he felt as if he were about to float away on a stiff breeze.

He led her to the dance floor, head high and feet light. *That's right*, his expression told Dan Harper when his friend raised an eyebrow at him, *I'm dancing with Laura Kemper.* But he kept the triumph bubbling within him well away from his grip on Miss Kemper's hand. He didn't want to scare her off—not when he'd come so far.

All right. He was all right, and he'd handle this with steady confidence. But then she swung around to face him, and Lord, the grace of her. She might be a better dancer than he was. He squared his shoulders, set his hand at her waist, the fit of her too perfect within his arms, and prayed for courage. Then he pushed them off to join the whirling crowd of dancers.

He kept it simple at first—his wobbly knees wouldn't be able to handle anything complicated. He focused on the feel of her under his hands, her body moving through space with his, the music directing them both. Dancing he knew. He might look too large and graceless everywhere else, but the dancing lessons his mother had insisted on ensured that he knew what he was about here.

Miss Kemper, however, looked quite steadily at his feet and not up at him as she was supposed to. Perhaps she wasn't such a good dancer. But he was holding her, they were moving together, and he was more than happy to simply take in her golden hair.

Perhaps she was watching his feet because she was worried he'd step on hers. To prove she had nothing to worry about, he tried to twirl her into a spin.

She stumbled into him, her feet tangling with his. He caught her, setting both hands at her waist to lift her up and over. Her hands came to cover his own as he put her back on her feet.

"I've got you." He tried to smile, but embarrassment caught at his throat, flamed on his face. He bit his lip as she lifted her hands from his. "I apologize, I shouldn't have knocked you over." *Idiot. Oaf.*

He let go of her. What kind of fool tripped the lady he was dancing with? No doubt she wanted to go back to Miss Moreno now.

She hit him with a smile, one that scrambled his mind like shaking an egg. "It's quite all right," she offered sweetly. "It was my fault. I'm certainly nowhere near as fine a dancer as you are." She lifted her hands. "Please, may we try again?"

Try again? Oh yes, he certainly wanted to try again. His skin went warm all over, then cold, then warm once more. "I promise we won't do anything like that again."

She was looking at the couples swirling past them. "If we're going to halt," she said uncertainly, "perhaps we should be out of everyone's path."

Mr. Howard sent them a nasty glance as he steered Mrs. Howard around them.

Right. Time to try again. Marcus grabbed her hand and pulled her back out, knowing he was being too hasty, too rough, but too nervous now to stop himself. Her gaze pointed straight back to the floor. This wasn't going as he'd planned—since he hadn't planned for it to be slowly sinking into disaster. He needed some way to recover this, to set things right.

He needed... *conversation.*

He swallowed a groan. He'd been so concerned with first asking her to dance, then actually dancing with her, that he'd forgotten about the talking to go along with it. His heart thrummed in his ears, loud enough that he wasn't certain he would hear her over it. He frowned down at the curls piled atop her head as he tried to think of something to say.

What did ladies like to talk about? Dresses? Sewing? What did his sisters talk about? He had five of them—he ought to remember *something* they'd said—

"How are your potatoes?" Miss Kemper asked the ground.

Potatoes. Those he knew. "They're doing well. It's still only spring, but we've had a good amount of rain, not too much, not too little. The true test will be when summer comes and the rain is gone. But I have some irrigation ideas—" *Stop. Just stop.* "I shouldn't be rambling on about it to a lady. You must be bored."

"I'm not bored at all," she assured him, but her voice was hollow. "Being the daughter and sister of shopkeepers, I know nothing of farming. It's interesting to hear about new subjects."

She didn't sound very interested. At least as far as he could tell, since she would only look at his feet.

"Well, as the ranchers tell me, it's only plants and dirt," he said.

"If it's only plants and dirt, why do so many fail at it?"

He grinned. "That's what I always say!" Perhaps she truly did understand. "You have to know when to plant, how to keep the vermin out, how to look for disease, how to plant your rows for drainage and sunlight. You don't simply throw plants some fodder and wait for them to fatten up."

She didn't answer, didn't look up.

Perhaps she didn't understand. Perhaps she didn't really care about farming. But that was all he knew.

Lord above, but this was disastrous. He could only talk about farming, and she could only look at their feet. He couldn't believe he'd taken so long to work up to this and it was all failing so spectacularly. He blinked hard, his feet moving without thought. He'd keep quiet for the rest of this, then deliver her back to Miss Moreno's side.

"It's been a lovely spring, hasn't it?" she asked.

The weather. He knew the weather. And he should have brought it up first. "The rain was good and we didn't have any late frosts," he answered. "So, yes, it's been a good spring." A thought came to him. "There's a field on my farm I've cleared but haven't planted. The poppies are coming up all through it and are just about to bloom. You might like to come by when they do."

Now that was inspired. She'd come to see the poppies, he'd show her the farm, and then... well, he'd figure out the *and then*.

"Of course," she said with a decided lack of enthusiasm. "Don't all ladies like flowers?"

She didn't sound as if she liked flowers. But she had said yes. Hadn't she?

"Oh, yes," she went on. "Catarina and I would love to see them. She's really the one you should be discussing farming with." She looked up at him—finally—and the blue of her eyes was all he could see. "For all that she makes her little jokes, she's quite the gardener. You two could spend hours and hours discussing plants." She smiled.

His feet slowed, then stopped. She was smiling at him—but she thought he should be talking to Catarina?

What exactly did she think this dance was about?

"I don't think we'll be doing that," he stammered.

Her smile widened. "Whyever not? I know Catarina might seem fast, but she's really not. And you couldn't find a person better suited to be a farm wife."

"Miss Moreno? You think *she* should be my wife?" His mouth wouldn't close properly after that.

Didn't Miss Kemper understand? He meant for *her* to be his wife. How she could have gotten such a crazed idea from their stilted dialogue?

"I don't think we ought to be stopped here," she pointed out. Again.

The dancing bit of this could go hang for all he cared, but he didn't dare use such language with Miss Kemper. Instead, he clasped her close to him—which wasn't so enjoyable after hearing that she thought he ought to be doing this with Miss Moreno—and resumed the steps.

"Why do you think I want to marry Miss Moreno?" A bit too pointed, but it seemed a queer notion for her to have seized upon.

"I should think it very obvious," she said reasonably, her gaze back on their feet. "This is the first time you've ever danced with anyone at one of these things. Why would you start dancing now unless you were looking for a wife?"

"You've noticed that I don't dance?" A warmth settled within him. He didn't think she'd taken any note of him.

"Well, you obviously do dance, and you do it quite well."

The warmth in his middle bloomed into heat.

"No, you choose not to dance. Except that now you do."

She'd gotten the part about looking for a wife right. She'd just misidentified the wife. Or so he thought. "You think I should marry Miss Moreno. Is that correct?"

She was mouthing something to herself. "Hmm? Oh, yes, but I'm not suggesting that you marry Catarina tomorrow, of course. Court her first and see if you suit. I could go over there with you to speak with her, if that would help."

If he weren't so in love with Miss Kemper, he might be tempted to be annoyed with her. What kind of a woman danced with a man, then assumed he should be courting someone else? This was even more muddling than when she smiled at him.

The music came to a climax before fading to nothing, the two of them slowing and stopping along with it. The rest of the couples burst into applause, but he merely set her back from him and searched her face. Was there any hope for him and his suit there? Or was she putting forth this nonsense about Miss Moreno to put him off as kindly as she could?

Her features were as lovely as ever but assumed an expression of mere politeness. Nothing more.

A flurry of motion from the edge of the room caught her eye and she turned. Miss Moreno was furiously waving her over, no doubt appalled Miss Kemper had danced so long with a "dirt grubber."

It was hopeless—it had all gone too terribly wrong. It was as if he were looking on an entire field of blight, a whole season of planting lost to fate. For heaven's sake, she thought he should be courting Miss Moreno and not herself.

He'd tried, after two years of waiting, and he'd failed. Lord, but this hurt, his arms remembering how she'd felt within them, watching the back of her as she looked toward the people she truly wanted to be with.

"I think I should head back over to Catarina," she said. "It looks like she needs me." She began to head off, waving at him over her shoulder. "Thank you for the dance."

A small spark of hope flared, traveled up his throat, and flew from his mouth. "Miss Kemper."

She turned back, her face open and inquiring.

He fisted his hands at his sides and kept his head high. He had braved a dragon to ask her to dance—he could ask for one thing more.

"Would you do me the honor of walking with me tomorrow after church?" Fast and stiff, but he'd said it. He'd made one last grasp.

She blinked as if he had said something unexpected. But then, slowly, she smiled. "Yes." She blinked again before repeating more firmly, "Yes. I'd be very pleased to walk with you after church tomorrow."

"Well." His chest swelled and his head spun as triumph surged through him. *She'd said yes.* "Well, I'll"—he stepped backward, bumping into someone behind him— "Sorry. Oh, not you, Miss Kemper! I'll, I'll see you tomorrow then."

Before this moment, he'd never understood how a heart could sing. How could a heart sing when it was only there to keep the time? But what else could explain the music filling his ears right now since the band had gone silent? It must be his heart singing.

Not even his first crop of potatoes had made him feel this giddy. But then again, he hadn't had to face down a dragon to harvest those potatoes.

The dragon in question was watching them from afar with narrowed eyes, no doubt trying to decide if she should roast him or not.

"Until tomorrow." Miss Kemper waggled her fingers at him, smiling shyly. Then she turned and walked away.

He met Miss Moreno's hard gaze for half a moment— not long enough to be rude. Just let her try to flame him with her sharp tongue. He was going walking with Miss Kemper tomorrow. That was all the armor he needed against a dragon.

Walking with Miss Kemper. That sounded so heavenly. How was he going to make it through church tomorrow, knowing what was waiting for him after?

"You going to dance, or are you going to stand there all night like a hound looking at a ham?"

"Huh?" He turned to find Dan Harper smirking at him, his eyes twinkling in his dark-skinned face.

"Music's starting up again and you're standing in the middle of the floor. I'd take you around myself, but then there's the tricky question of which one of us is going to lead."

"Very amusing. I'm moving right now."

"Why don't you move on out to the woodshed with me and we'll have ourselves a nip of whiskey with the other fellows?"

"Sounds good." Marcus had done what he'd set out to do this evening—a little celebration was in order.

The night air instantly chilled him, reminding him that spring, for all its sunny days, still had a cold bite. Strange how he hadn't noticed how warm it had been when they were dancing. He only hoped he hadn't perspired much.

"So you finally did it." Dan was smirking again, but there was a fond twist that lessened the sting.

"I don't know what you mean." Marcus aimed for dignified but only hit starchy.

"Come on." Dan scoffed. "You've been mooning over Laura Kemper since you settled here. It's taken about two years, but you finally did it."

Marcus grasped the whiskey bottle Larsen was offering, the glass cold in his palm as the drink warmed his throat, then his stomach. The liquor was kept strictly away from the dance in order to avoid the wrath of the Ladies' Temperance League. As long as they never saw a bottle, they were willing to overlook their men disappearing outside for some "fresh air."

"What did Marcus finally do?" Luke Crivelli asked. "Come to his senses and give up on farming?"

The circle of men guffawed while Marcus only smiled. When he'd first moved to Cabrillo, he'd been put off by their jokes, thinking they meant to make him feel unwelcome. But as time passed, he realized it was exactly the opposite: that was how they welcomed him. Everyone had a fault the entire town would jest about—his happened to be that he was a farmer.

"Noooo," Dan crowed. "He finally spoke to Laura Kemper. Hell, he didn't just speak to her." Dan paused dramatically, waiting until he had every man's attention. "He actually *danced with her.*"

Hoots and hollers rose from the circle, and a few men even slapped Marcus on the back. He ducked his head, wishing his face weren't flaming with embarrassment like a girl's. But under all that discomfort, pleasure glowed. He hadn't only danced with her—he'd have hours tomorrow alone with her, the two of them enjoying a spring Sunday together.

"I guess we'd better book the church for the wedding," Luke said.

Marcus dug the toe of his boot into the dirt. If only he could think of something witty to say. If only his tongue weren't numb from embarrassment—and whiskey.

"A man could do worse," Dan mused.

Worse? A man couldn't do better.

Luke frowned. "I suppose so. I never really gave much thought to little Laura, to tell the truth. Of course, she's always with Catarina Moreno, and we all know it's hard to look past Catarina."

The entire circle murmured their agreement.

Marcus kept quiet.

"I wonder who'll finally catch that girl," Luke said.

"Whoever marries Catarina Moreno, he'll be one lucky bastard," someone offered.

That was entirely too far. "I've never thought Miss Moreno was quite so fine as all that," Marcus bit out.

Every eyebrow shot up.

"Are you telling me," Luke said, his voice dripping incredulity, "that if you had the choice between Catarina Moreno and Laura Kemper, you'd pick Miss Kemper?"

Luke made the choice sound as if it were between Helen of Troy and Medusa.

"Yes, I would," Marcus said stoutly. "Miss Kemper is a fine, beautiful lady with a kind spirit." Marcus felt like a knight of old, defending his ladylove's honor. "Miss Moreno is a flirt and much too high in the instep for her own good."

A few knowing nods then.

"Catarina would be a handful," Dan agreed. "A man wouldn't have a restful marriage with her."

"But what a handful." Luke sighed. "I'd happily die of exhaustion."

Marcus's mouth screwed up as if he'd bitten into a lemon. He'd never understood how a whole town of men could overlook a lady such as Miss Kemper just because her best friend liked to flaunt herself. It made him mad enough to spit.

"All right, boys," Dan said, catching sight of his face. "We'd better stop insulting Miss Kemper's honor or it'll be pistols at dawn for all of us."

"Oh, Marcus," Luke said, laughter bursting at the seams of his voice, "we were only joshing with you. We know how lovely Miss Laura is. You going to take her for a buggy ride tomorrow?"

"I don't have a buggy or else I would." He smiled, re-membering that little wave of hers as she'd walked away. The shy smile she'd directed at him. "We're going walk-ing tomorrow after church."

"Ooh," the entire circle chorused.

His face flamed again, the heat spreading to his neck and ears this time. "It's only a walk. I wouldn't dare take any liberties with Miss Kemper."

Dan laughed and shook his head. "I swear, Marcus, you're more proper than a preacher. I hope Miss Kemper isn't expecting anything, or she's going to be mighty disappointed."

Marcus fervently hoped she wouldn't be disappointed at all.

~~~

He was a surprisingly good dancer.

From his size and retiring demeanor, Laura never would have guessed dancing came so easily to Mr. Gries. Not that she'd had an occasion to think about his skills at dancing before, since she'd never seen him do it.

But he was so accomplished at it, his feet moving without thought, that she'd felt clumsy in his arms. She'd had to watch her feet the entire time to keep from stumbling.

His attempts at conversation had not been even half so graceful as his dancing though. He seemed almost... *afraid* to speak with her. Why that should be, she'd no idea. She certainly hadn't the kind of face that pushed men into speechlessness.

But it *had* been nice, moving with him in those moments as the music urged them along. She hadn't been expecting much this evening—she'd sit with Catarina, they'd chat about everything and nothing, men would cluster around them, pestering Catarina for attention and a dance, and then they'd all go home.

But it was better than sitting in sullen silence with her parents in the back rooms of the store.

"Well," Catarina said with a huff of distaste, "that was interesting."

"It was nice," Laura responded out of reflexive politeness. She pondered for a moment—it had been nice, now that the experience was settling a bit.

"So strange," Catarina went on. "He's never said more than two words to you, never dances with anyone…" She gave Laura a slow, sidelong glance. "If he asked you to dance and for a walk, he must be sweet on you."

A denial leapt to the edge of her tongue, but she shut her teeth on it. At first she'd thought he'd asked her to dance because he couldn't work up the nerve to ask Catarina, his true target. Certainly that had happened before, a young man sidling up to Laura as preparation for the challenge of her beautiful friend.

But Mr. Gries's reaction to her offer of help—and his asking her to walk after church—was proof that he had little, if any, interest in Catarina.

Perhaps he *was* sweet on Laura.

She released a slow, silent breath, trying to blow that thought away. He'd never shown her any considered attention before. Their exchanges were usually limited to *Hello* and *How are you,* making tonight's chat the longest they'd ever had. And he'd proved he was no conversationalist.

She ought to have told him no when he'd asked to walk with her.

All the reasons she should have crowded her mind. Her parents, sitting alone in those back rooms, never leaving even for church. Poor Rose, her sister-in-law, stuck with the two of them all afternoon while they rained their petty abuses on her head. And herself, stuck alongside them on a pretty Sunday, breathing in a cloud of misery instead of the fresh spring air.

She should have said no. She owed it to her parents and Rose, especially after the freedom of tonight.

So why had she said yes?

"I think you're wrong, Catarina." Laura frowned at Marcus's back as he disappeared outside. "He only wanted to dance with someone." *And walk with them after church.*

Catarina shook her head. "Why is it so unlikely that he's interested in you?"

"Mmm." Laura slanted her friend a look. "Perhaps because most of the boys here are interested in you and not me?"

The other girl waved that off. "I fail to see why. And I fail to see why you aren't interested in getting married."

"Not every young lady is as obsessed with marriage as you are. Besides, with my parents, and Frank, and Rose…" She deliberately let her voice die away. The last thing she wanted to do on her night of freedom was talk about her family situation.

"As I've said before, you simply need to find a husband wealthy enough to take in you and your parents."

Laura slanted her friend another look.

"And of course, one you fancy as well. If he even exists." Catarina muttered that last bit.

"Or," Laura countered, "I could simply go on as I have and help Rose and Frank care for my parents without fretting about marriage."

Her friend wasn't listening—she was staring at the open barn door Marcus had disappeared through. "You know," she said slowly, "I think it might be time for you to look for a husband."

"I thought you didn't approve of Marcus."

"I don't. You can do much better."

"How is that? He's kind, and…" And what? *He likes to talk about potatoes.* "And he's a very fine dancer," she finished firmly.

Catarina released a puff of scorn. "If he's such a fine dancer, why doesn't he ever dance?"

Good question. One Mr. Gries hadn't answered when she'd asked him. "I think he's bashful."

Catarina rolled her eyes. "Bashful and a dirt-poor farmer. Even if he were wealthy enough, can you imagine what would happen when *bashful* meets your mother's ill humor?"

Laura had to concede that point. Her mother would demolish the bashful Mr. Gries with her bitter tongue—not that Laura would ever bring him to her family's table.

"No." Catarina tapped her chin thoughtfully, taking on a pensive air that sent trepidation rolling through Laura's belly. "I think that a doctor husband might be just the thing. Do you know the doctor at the sanatorium over in Pine Ridge?"

"You know that I don't. A doctor?"

"Yes, him. I wonder what his name is. Doctors are quite well off—they should be, with their fees—and he would be a help with your father."

Laura doubted that very much. Doctor Blackmun himself had said there was nothing to be done about her father's condition.

"You should use your walk with Marcus tomorrow to practice," Catarina went on. "It will be good to have a bit of experience enticing a man if you want to marry this doctor."

Marry the doctor? Laura most certainly did not want to do that. She didn't want to marry anyone. "That doesn't sound very nice," she protested. Poor Mr. Gries didn't deserve to be used for sport.

"You aren't truly sweet on him, are you?" Catarina asked, sharp as an insect's bite.

"It doesn't matter if I am or not," Laura pointed out. "It's unkind to use him as practice. He's not a straw target."

"Why did you agree to go walking with him?"

Not because she was sweet on him, that was certain. The real reason was rather unflattering—but Catarina knew Laura's facade of the dutiful daughter was sometimes just that—only a false front. "The thought of being cooped up in those rooms all day on a Sunday..." She shrugged and knew her smile was sad, but it was the best she could summon. "I only wanted one Sunday for myself. I suppose I am unkind."

Catarina's face was a study in sympathy with a touch of pity. "If you marry that doctor, you'll have every Sunday for yourself."

Perhaps her friend was right—perhaps she should be looking for a husband. But the thought made her tired. Even more tired than the thought of returning home to those rooms behind the mercantile, at the thought of years and years and years of caring for her parents. It was her duty, and she would honor it, but Lord, it exhausted a person.

"If it were your father," she asked gently, "would you selfishly want every Sunday for yourself?"

Catarina touched her hand, a gentle tap of understanding. "Just think on it. And while you're going walking tomorrow, I'll see what I can find out about this doctor. Simply asking around can't hurt," she added at Laura's glance.

Laura lifted her brows. "Are you going to find out his name? Perhaps if he has a wife?"

Her gentle sarcasm didn't deter her friend. "Well, yes, but other things too. It's much easier to entice a man if you know something about him."

She supposed Catarina would know. But truly, it was time to stop all this foolishness—she wasn't marrying any doctor. She was about to tell Catarina exactly that when the expression on her friend's face shut her mouth.

Catarina's mood over the past few months had slowly become more forced, more desperate. Laura privately worried that her friend might be tipping ever so gradually into hysteria. She was so brittle these days a hammer tap might shatter the shell of her. Yet now her face was animated, even amused.

What harm could it do, this lark of a doctor beau? Catarina was quite persuasive with men, but Laura couldn't imagine even her convincing a doctor to come all the way to Cabrillo to court a young lady.

She'd go for a walk with Marcus tomorrow, Catarina would tease her about it and the doctor for a few weeks, and then life would go on much as it always had.

Laura gave a long glance at the dance floor. At least she would always have the memory of that surprisingly fine dance with Mr. Gries.

CHAPTER TWO

THE FIRST CONGREGATIONAL CHURCH OF Cabrillo looked as it did most Sunday mornings. Sunlight streamed in from the high-set windows, painting the walls blinding white. Normally that light would have filled Marcus with a solemn reverence, but today the buzz of his own thoughts blended with the hum of his neighbors' conversations to make him itchy and out of sorts.

He glanced over the milling crowd again, tapping an impatient hand against his leg. Laura still wasn't here yet. He was in the back corner of the church, the best vantage point in the whole place—he couldn't have missed her.

His fingers fished out his pocket watch without thought, his thumb snapping open the catch. Two minutes until services started. He slid the watch back.

Wait, was that right? He pulled it out again, flicked it open as his leg jiggled with the anxiety bubbling in him. Yes, only two minutes left.

He drummed his fingers against the back of the pew, fighting the urge to go look outside for her. She would come. She'd promised last night. Miss Kemper was not the kind of girl to go back on a promise.

Perhaps she had though. His chest and throat went tight. She had said yes last night... but calling their conversation awkward would have been too kind. She might have reconsidered after a night's reflection. His leg took up that jerky rhythm again.

If she'd changed her mind, he didn't know what he would do.

His leg slowed, then stopped, and his head drooped toward his knees as he imagined waiting through the entire service. Waiting for a lady who wasn't coming. That might be harder than finding the nerve to dance with her had been.

Rose and Frank. There were Rose and Frank Kemper, making their way into a pew. He almost called out to them, so great was his relief. Laura would be coming up behind them. She had to be. Any moment now and he'd see her. In her Sunday best, her golden curls brushing the pink of her cheeks—she might even favor him with a shy smile as she went by.

Only, she didn't. He kept his neck craned and his gaze right on the church door, but she never appeared.

She wasn't coming.

He sank into the pew as that realization crushed him. The reverend's words washed over his ears without penetrating, Marcus's focus solely on his own clasped hands and the curious buzzing in his ears, a buzzing that sounded exactly like severe disappointment would.

Perhaps... He took his pocket watch out once more. Fifteen minutes late. He replaced the watch, then very carefully patted his pocket. Linking his hands together in his lap, he stared down at them as a curious hollowness filled his chest.

What could have gone wrong? He would have sworn she'd have simply said no if she didn't want to go. She'd have done it very kindly, but it would have unmistakably been a *no*.

She had said yes. He had to hold on to that, to the feel of her in his arms last night, the warmth of her smile as she'd accepted his invitation. She could not have fabricated such a smile.

Which left him with the fact that she'd said yes but was not here in church.

Marcus wasn't one for puzzles or riddles—only this mystery was one he desperately wanted to solve. The future of his heart was at stake.

If she wasn't in church, she must be at home. Goodness, he hoped she wasn't ill. He could ask Frank if she was all right, but they were clear on the other side of the church. And if the preacher held to his usual schedule, they were in here for at least another hour.

An hour of wondering, worrying—that was quite a stretch of time. He shifted in his seat, careful not to disturb those seated next to him. A man as big as he was always had to watch out for others.

If Laura were ill, they would have called for the doctor. But, no, there was Dr. Blackmun in the third row, already fast asleep.

Perhaps she wasn't ill, just feeling a bit poorly. Yes, that was probably it—Frank would no doubt convey a message to him after services to that effect. It was a shame they wouldn't be able to go for their walk today, but there was always next Sunday.

But what if she was feeling worse? What if, even now, she was all alone, burning up with a fever, wishing someone, anyone, would come and call the doctor?

His fists clenched in his lap.

This was foolishness. She was fine. He had to sit here and wait until the service was over. Frank would explain everything then. A man couldn't go haring off in the middle of church to visit a young unmarried lady alone. He needed to stay right where he was, planted in this pew.

That was exactly what he'd do. Stay right here and attend to the sermon.

He shot up so quickly he startled everyone to the left and right of him. "Sorry," he muttered. The reverend paused for a moment, peering at him as if Marcus had just arrived from the moon. Marcus gave him a weak smile, then headed for the door. As he inched past the folks in the pew, Widow Sand's expression told him exactly where she thought he was headed in the afterlife for this kind of behavior. But he pressed on.

The streets were empty when he emerged into the bright spring sunlight, blinking hard against it until he settled his hat on his head. Thank goodness no one was around to see what a fool he was being. Well, except for everyone in church, but it was too late to do anything about that.

Slowly, slowly, he chided himself as he walked to Kemper's Mercantile, his thighs tight with the urge to break into a run. He mustn't go tearing through town like a madman or arrive at her door sweating and out of breath. Calm. Rational. A good marriage prospect. That was how he had to appear.

By the time he rounded the corner of the mercantile building and came within sight of the back porch, his breathing had a slight hitch to it and his leg muscles were tingling.

She was there. Eyes closed, head leaning against the back of her chair, throat one long, pure line stretching from her chin to her collar. He slowed and approached quietly. Mustn't wake her or startle her. Especially if she was ill. But her cheeks were their usual ivory, no hint of the flush of fever in them, thank goodness.

He stopped short, wanting to smack himself in the forehead. Dang it all, he should have brought her some flowers. The fields were bursting with them, and it would have been a moment's work to pick a little bouquet. He could still sneak back and get some...

Some harsh words from the porch signaled that he'd been spotted. It wasn't English, but sounded... German? Only not quite.

His mouth went dry and dread settled in his chest as he made his way to the porch, the sheer stupidity of his plan finally reaching his brain. He'd left church to call on an unmarried lady. While her brother was away. He'd look the veriest scoundrel when he explained what he was up to. The opposite of a good marriage prospect.

A deep gust of a sigh left his lips. Too late now—he ought to have thought of that in church, before he'd done this fool thing.

He was well and truly trapped.

~~~

Escape wasn't going to happen for her this Sunday.

Laura pulled at the neckline of her second-best dress, trying to swallow past the tight spot in her throat. Rose bustled past her, clearing the breakfast dishes, her feet and hands light as she did so. *Her* feet were light because this was Frank and Rose's Sunday to go to church.

It was not Laura's Sunday for church. Instead, she must stay in with her parents. And miss a walk with Mr. Gries.

Seeing how happy Rose was, Laura couldn't bear to ask to go instead. It would have been too cruel, because Rose would agree without a second thought.

Life was unfair, but it seemed particularly unfair today.

Mr. Gries was sure to be disappointed, but no doubt he'd find some other young lady to ask. With his warm brown eyes, his shy smile nestled in his beard, his steady, strong hands... he had only to ask, and a new young lady would be on his arm.

The trouble was, she would very much like to be that lady.

She'd thought of their dance all last night. If she hadn't been so worried about where her feet were supposed to go, she might have enjoyed it more, reveled in that sensation of floating on the music with an accomplished partner.

She sighed silently, rising from the table and leaving the rest of her cold tea.

"Mother, are you finished?" she asked in Dutch.

Her mother waved an irritable hand toward her nearly full plate. "I suppose so," she responded in the same language. "I don't see how I can be expected to eat this American cooking. I only wish I were well so I could cook us some proper, nourishing food."

Laura wished her mother were well too. Mrs. Kemper hadn't always been like this, so irritable and listless.

She'd been stern, to be sure, but Laura had never felt unloved. Once her father had sickened... Well, after that, everything had changed.

"Rose's cooking is quite nice, Mother." It was useless to defend Rose against her mother's attacks, but she still kept at it. Better a futile gesture than none at all.

She turned to her father at the foot of the table. "Father, are you finished?"

Her father's face was the usual blank mask, no hint of emotion written there. His right hand was flat upon the table, occasionally spasming involuntarily. The left hand—the weak hand—was hidden under the table, curled into a useless claw.

"Yes," he slurred.

She took both plates into the kitchen, passing Frank as he came into the dining room.

"Do you want to move, Father?" he asked loudly.

Laura shook her head. Her father could hear quite well, but her brother insisted on raising his voice, as if volume alone could shear through the disease that had taken hold. Creeping paralysis, the doctor had called it.

"Suppose so," her father answered.

Laura came back into the dining room as her father slowly rose with Frank's help, every movement a struggle to achieve. Her mother watched the whole process with sharp, narrowed eyes.

"Be careful," she snapped when Father came near the sideboard.

"I always am, Mother." Resigned—which was usual for Frank these days.

The first sign something was afflicting her father had been his sudden, unexplained lack of balance. After one particularly terrifying fall, in which he'd gashed his head, he'd finally admitted to the weakness plaguing his legs and left arm.

From then on, her father had progressively worsened.

"Let's go sit in the parlor." Her mother flicked a thin hand toward the doorway.

"Oh!" Laura couldn't bite down her protest quick enough.

Her mother turned to her, annoyance sparking off her ice-blue eyes.

"I thought it might be nice to sit on the porch," Laura explained, "since it's such a fine day. The fresh air might do us all some good." She clasped her hands before her, praying this show of demureness would appease her mother.

"Mmm." Her father rocked from side to side as he shuffled in a small circle to turn toward the front door. "Porch sounds good."

"Help your father, Frank." Her mother's words were as tart as green fruit. She would be especially difficult now Laura had overridden her, but it was a worthy price to pay to escape the confinement of their living quarters.

It began as soon they were settled on the porch.

"There's too much wind. I can hardly keep my knitting in my hands, the wind is pulling it so. Laura, switch places with me; you're in a sheltered spot."

Laura did as she was told, switching back a few minutes later when her mother declared her original seat had been better protected after all. Through it, her father sat expressionless, only the tremors in his hand proving he hadn't turned to stone.

"What trials we have to bear, your father and I," her mother said to the knitting in her lap.

Laura rubbed her forehead with the tips of her fingers as hard as she dared. Her father was the one who was ill, but her mother insisted on sinking down with him, the loyal wife to the bitter end.

At the first signs of her father's illness, her mother had been frantic for a cure, even in the face of the doctor's assertion nothing could be done. But the dozens of patent medicines her mother had forced down her father's throat had only made him feel drunk.

When one such potion from a passing quack had made her father vomit for three days, he'd told her mother enough and refused any more. From then on, her mother had sunk into bitterness as surely as her father was sinking into paralysis.

Nothing was preventing her mother from leaving these rooms, nothing except her own stubborn refusal to leave her husband's side. No doubt when they laid their father to rest, their mother would insist on being placed in the casket with him.

"If only we had a grandchild to comfort us in such troubles," her mother went on. "But, of course, that stupid girl your brother married can't even do that."

Laura felt the old familiar leadenness settle on her. How many times had they had this conversation? How many more times would they have to have it?

"It's not Rose's fault." Again with the futile gestures. "It saddens her as much as it does you."

"Humph. If your brother had listened to us and married that nice girl we had picked out instead, he'd have plenty of children. I just know your father and I are sickening from her cooking. If only I were well enough to cook again."

Laura pulled at her neckline, trying to loosen it without unbuttoning it. Her mother was perfectly able to cook whatever she pleased. It was perversity itself, the way her mother railed against Rose's housekeeping yet never lifted a finger to help.

"If you felt up to it," she offered, "I could help you with the cooking one of these evenings. Then you could have whatever you liked." Even to her own ears, her voice sounded flat.

"I wish you could spend a day in my shoes, Laura, so you would know how absurd that suggestion is."

"Mother's right," her father put in. "Frank should have married the other. Would have been much better for all of us."

"Why, she can't even speak Dutch!" her mother continued. "Only German. I can't tell you how terrible it is to have to speak to your daughter-in-law in a foreign tongue."

Considering her mother mostly spoke Dutch, the better to exclude Rose, Laura didn't think it could be so terrible. "You could have learned English." Her irritation snuck in there. "Then you could speak with everyone here, not just Frank and me."

"My own daughter, speaking to me so!" The shock on her mother's face was so purely false Laura almost sniggered. "After all we did for you, to raise and educate you, such insolence is quite wounding. You're meant to be our comfort in our old age, but I must say, I don't feel very comforted right now."

"I am sorry, Mother," she mumbled. Not as contrite as she should have been, but her patience was thin and her well of sympathy was drained.

Her mother simply huffed and went back to her knitting.

Laura turned her face to the front of the porch, closing her eyes as she savored the fresh air stroking her face. The wind pulled a few strands of hair free from her twist, tickling her with them. She filled her lungs with the sweet scent of spring flowers that were bursting forth in every part of Cabrillo.

Yes, it was worth facing her mother's sharp tongue to be able to bask in the sun like this.

Two more hours until Rose and Frank returned from church.

And after that, she had only the rest of her parents' natural lives to get through.

No, she would not think on those long years to endure, watching her mother decline right along with her father. Not today, not with spring singing with flowers and warmth and greenness. And she wouldn't think of a certain farmer, of her hand tucked in his arm, his bulk next to her as they walked through the melody nature was crafting.

But her plans to not think of Mr. Gries were foiled by the man himself coming around the corner of the mercantile.

CHAPTER THREE

MISS KEMPER'S BLUE EYES WIDENED at the sight of him, trapping Marcus in the force of her gaze. And her obvious shock.

Why had he done such a silly thing as leaving the church in search of her? If she hadn't wanted to take that walk, he'd just caused her untold embarrassment, appearing like this.

"Mr. Gries?" A hint of guilt there—but no suggestion of an unwelcome chill.

The older lady on the porch snapped out something to Miss Kemper—it wasn't quite German, but it was close. The older man simply stared impassively.

These must be Laura's parents. He'd hoped their first meeting might have gone better than this, considering he wanted to marry their daughter.

Well, there was still time for a show of the manners his mother had drilled into him. He took off his hat and twisted it in his hands. "Miss Kemper, I... I... How are you?"

A smile teased at the corners of her mouth. "I'm well." She gestured to the couple on the porch. "These are my parents."

He nodded respectfully. "I'm Marcus Gries. Pleased to meet you, ma'am, sir."

The lady kept her sour expression and the gentleman remained impassive. Marcus wasn't erasing his first impression that easily, it seemed.

Laura turned to them and translated what he'd said into... *Dutch.* That's what it was—Dutch. The lady made a scornful noise, while the man's blank stare never flickered.

"They're pleased to meet you too, Mr. Gries," she said to him when she was finished.

Considering neither had said anything that could be construed as a greeting, Marcus doubted that.

Miss Kemper stood, her whole frame rigid. He never should have come. Her obvious distress at the sight of him was a knife to his heart. "Mr. Gries," she said, "I am so sorry I couldn't accompany you today, but I completely forgot it was my turn to stay home." Her fine brows drew together. "I should have asked Frank to tell you, and I feel terrible you came all this way."

"That's all right, Miss Kemper; it was nothing to come out here. When I didn't see you in church this morning, I worried you might be ill, and I wanted to be sure you were well." His nose and ears flamed as he said it. It sounded doubly silly out loud with her parents scowling at him.

But her answering smile was so warmly genuine he found himself smiling in return. Perhaps it hadn't been so silly.

"I'm touched you thought of me," she said, "but I assure you, I'm quite fine."

They smiled at one another for a moment, no doubt looking addlepated, but it was one of the nicest moments of his life.

She hadn't meant to disappoint him. She was smiling. All was well.

Mrs. Kemper bit off something harsh, a phrase that must have meant *What does he want?* judging by the suspicious cast of her eyes. They were light and clear, completely unlike the smoky blue of Miss Kemper's.

Miss Kemper turned to her mother, her voice low as she answered, her fists buried in her skirts. But her voice stayed steady as she replied to her mother's increasingly agitated phrases.

His spirits sank as they went back and forth for a time, Miss Kemper winding up tighter and tighter with every word her mother said.

He ought to go; it was clear her mother didn't want him around. He'd made certain Miss Kemper was fine. There was always next Sunday for their walk.

That would be enough to get him through the week. It would have to be.

Then Mr. Kemper spoke.

Marcus noticed his hands lay uselessly in his lap and his words were slurred, but the older man sounded as if he was usually obeyed. Mrs. Kemper settled back into a sullen silence at his words, the pinch of her mouth speaking to her unvoiced feelings.

Miss Kemper turned to him, and the smile that lit her mouth and eyes—her whole face—was as dazzling as a flash of sun peeking through spring storm clouds. He could only blink against such a smile.

She spoke the finest words he'd ever heard, better than any of the poetry he'd had to read in school:

"Mr. Gries, would you still like to take that walk with me?"

~~~

"What does that man want?"

Her mother's tone was the same as she'd use to complain about a skunk on the porch.

Every muscle in Laura's body clenched instinctively, but she kept control of her voice. "He asked me last night if I would go walking with him. I agreed, forgetting I needed to stay home today."

"You agreed to go walking with this man without asking our permission? When did you become such a fast young lady, Laura?"

If she thought that was fast, her mother would faint to see some of the tricks Catarina pulled. "I was going to ask you," she said, "but then I remembered I wouldn't be able to go."

"He needs to leave then." Her mother made a shooing motion of her hand, as if Mr. Gries were a loose chicken. "Imagine that, coming around the back of the store like a sneak thief! No doubt he thought to catch you alone."

"I wasn't able to tell him I couldn't make it, and he thought I might be ill. There's nothing sinister about it." It was rather sweet, in truth. She hadn't been fussed over like this since she was a child.

"He's seen you're well and cannot go walking with him," her mother groused. "Why isn't he leaving?"

"Enough."

At her father's sharp command, both she and her mother turned to face him, no doubt wearing identical pop-mouthed expressions.

"Go walking. We'll be fine until Frank returns." Her father's expression was its usual mask, but his eyes sparked with—encouragement? Happiness? It had been so long since there had been any kind of emotion on his face she couldn't tell.

Her mother's reaction was ridiculously easy to read, the discontent written clearly in the tight lines around her eyes and mouth as she bent over her knitting.

But she could go.

The sense of freedom rushing through Laura was so potent that her vision went gray for a moment. She turned to Mr. Gries to tell him the good news.

The poor man was clutching his hat so tightly it would never recover. He must have guessed at the topic being discussed, even though he gave no indication he'd understood what had been said.

She smiled, near drunk on the promise of freedom for a few hours and a little amused at the picture he made. Who would have guessed such a darling man was hidden beneath his overalls?

"Mr. Gries," she said, delighted to be able to keep to her promise to him, "would you still like to take that walk with me?"

He unwound at that, his body going longer and leaner as the tension left him, and he smiled.

The way it transformed his rather ordinary features set her on her heels. That smile said she'd given him everything he'd ever wanted. It made him look... handsome. Desirable. A warmth unthreaded deep within her core to wrap itself around her heart.

"I can't think of anything I would like better." His deep voice practically licked at her ears, rough as a cat's tongue. She almost shivered with it.

Perhaps she was becoming feverish. She certainly felt warmer now he was smiling at her so.

"Let… let me just get my hat." She waggled her fingers at him and rushed into the house as fast as dignity would allow.

Catching sight of herself in the mirror on the way out, she pulled up short, hardly recognizing the girl in the mirror. The color in her cheeks was high, but not fevered, and her eyes were actually sparkling. She could see the sparkles for herself.

Most surprising of all was the smile she wore. She didn't think she'd ever seen herself smile so widely, at least not since her father had sickened. Now her smile took up half her face, crossing the line from giddy to simply ridiculous. But she couldn't make the muscles in her face relax. She felt too—*happy*.

He'd worried about her. He'd been concerned she was ill.

Laura hadn't allowed herself to be ill in years. Such privileges were reserved solely for her mother. And her father—well, that wasn't an illness. That was a slow theft of life.

He hadn't left church and come all this way for *Catarina*. He'd done that for *her*. Plain little Laura Kemper.

She tripped down the porch steps, almost laughing when she saw Mr. Gries wore a smile as wide as hers.

"I'll return in an hour or so," she called back to her parents.

Mr. Gries held his arm to her as she approached, gallant as any knight in a novel. She set her hand in the crook of his elbow, noting how it swallowed up her little hand. Yet he was so gentle for such a big man, moving as if he was always aware of the damage he could cause with a careless movement.

He pulled out a pocket watch and checked it. "If you need to be home in one hour, we'll need to turn back at exactly 10:13." He nodded once, then replaced the watch, patting his pocket as he did.

They walked through the deserted town in silence. The sun's rays were warm while the breeze still held a hint of winter. Just the usual contrasts of spring in the air as summer and winter fought for control.

Their gaits were slightly out of rhythm so that she barely brushed against him with every other step. She caught hints of his scent every time she got close, that same smell of clean skin he'd worn at the dance. Here in the sunshine, she noted how well it suited him, nothing artful or masking about it.

"Your family hasn't been in Cabrillo very long," he remarked.

Oh dear. They'd need to make conversation, not just walk. She only hoped it wouldn't be as painful as last night. "About two years now." She cast about for something other than her family to talk about. Potatoes were the only thing that came to mind.

Or perhaps they could talk about *his* family.

"You grew up in the valley?" she asked hastily before he could continue on.

"I did, but as far as folks in Cabrillo are concerned, it isn't the same as being raised here."

"It is a very tight-knit town." That was something she'd never considered before, that the two of them were both outsiders here, having been born somewhere else.

"Where's your family from?"

She took a moment, trying to decide what to reveal and what not. "My parents are from the Netherlands. They arrived in Santa Barbara after a few years in America. My father ran a mercantile, as Frank does now." She left out how they ended up in Cabrillo. Others' misfortunes never made for pleasant conversation.

"You grew up in Santa Barbara? Right next to the ocean?" A hint of wistfulness crept into his voice. "What was it like?"

She thought back to the time by the coast. It seemed like someone else's life, carefree in a way she'd taken for granted. "The seasons weren't so extreme. It was more like early spring all the time, sometimes cool and wet, sometimes warm and dry, but never hot or cold." She paused, remembering the cool fog that had often enveloped Santa Barbara, tangy with the taste of sea salt. "And it always smelled like the ocean."

"I've never seen the ocean."

She looked at him in surprise. But of course, what need would a farmer have with the ocean?

"The ocean is so vast you can't see the end of it. And the hum of the waves is always present, never ceasing. It's actually quite like the mountains," she mused. "You can't see the end of them either, and the noise of the wind through the pines sounds quite a bit like waves. They certainly both make you feel very small."

He pursed his lips and stared at the ranges turned green by the spring rains, the sunlight tangling in his short beard. "They do make you feel small, don't they? Especially living so close to them. Of course, you can see them down in the valley too, but they're almost too far away to be real there."

He'd just said more words in that little speech than she'd heard from him in the past two years. Who knew he was so... thoughtful?

Thoughtful and caring, and yes, rather handsome. She dropped her head and gave a tiny shake. It was only a walk. She mustn't build cloud castles.

"Do you miss living in the valley?"

"No, I can't say that I miss it. When I first moved up here, it was hard, fixing up the farm. There was a lot of brush to be cleared—still is—and irrigation to set up and seed potatoes to plant. Down in the valley, there was always someone to help, but up here, there's only me. In some ways I enjoyed it since it was all my own work, my own decisions—I wasn't just another cog in the Gries family farm. But I also sometimes hated it because there wasn't anyone to share it with."

The warm thread that had wrapped round her heart gave a sharp tug at his words. Yes, she understood loneliness.

He slowed as they came to a fork in the road. If they went right, they'd be on the road that snaked down the mountain face and into the valley. If they headed left, they'd go toward Rancho Moreno, Strawberry Creek, and Mount Portola.

He pulled the pocket watch out again. "There's not enough time to go all the way to the creek, and I imagine the wildflowers will be the same no matter which road we take." His expression was so purely solicitous it made her feel a bit weepy. "Which direction would you like to go?"

Now the tears were truly pressing. It was enough that he'd taken her for a walk on this fine spring day. But to ask where she wanted to go? It had been so long since someone asked her what she wanted to do that the simple choice nearly overwhelmed her.

"I'd... I'd like to head down the road to the valley. I often visit Catarina at Rancho Moreno, but I never walk down the valley road."

"Then that's the way we'll go."

The fields along the road were dotted with little purple and white flowers that nodded with the wind as small brown birds darted among them, no doubt looking for insects. A rabbit scampered across the road in front of them.

"Your nemesis has come out to greet us," she said, pointing at the rabbit.

He laughed. "Rabbits don't eat potato plants. They're poisonous."

"Really? I don't know anything about farming. Does your family grow potatoes in the valley?"

"Oh, they grow about everything down there, since the water company provides the irrigation."

"But there's no water company here," she said. "So how do you water your plants?"

"Well, there's the pond that abuts my land. I use that. I have to be careful how many acres I plant, although I have some ideas for digging deeper wells to provide more water."

It all sounded more complicated than she expected. "It's not easy farming up here, is it?"

His smile was rueful. "My family thought I was crazy to try it. But I had to get away from them while still being close." He frowned and shook his head. "That doesn't make any sense."

"No," she said slowly. "I think I understand what you mean. You can love your family, love them dearly, but still feel like they're suffocating you." Her face flushed as she realized what she'd said. It made her family sound so awful when really they weren't. She did truly love them. No doubt he was appalled at what she'd said.

But when she peeped at his face, it was thoughtful, considering.

"Yes, it's exactly like that," he said. "My family is dearer to me than anything, but if I heard one more time about how I couldn't do this or that because I was the baby and didn't know what I was doing—well, I would have screamed."

It was hard to imagine this man as anyone's baby. With every brush of her body against his, she was reminded again of how solid and strong he was. The bulk of him seemed as unyielding as that of Mount Portola in the distance, towering over everything in sight.

But even he could feel small and insignificant, and even he could want to escape his family while remaining close.

The thread around her heart tugged sharply again.

He pulled out his pocket watch one last time, sighing when he read it. "I'm afraid it's 10:27, Miss Kemper," he said, resignation running deep in his voice. "We'll be late getting back. I hope it won't cause you any trouble."

She had to smile at his fastidiousness. "Perhaps you would like to call me Laura?"

A strange sort of buzzing went through her when he smiled back, starting in her ears, then spreading throughout her entire body. It was warm and tingly and strangely addictive. She hoped he'd smile at her like that in the future so she could experience the sensation again.

"I'd like that very much. Please call me Marcus."

"Marcus." Of course, she'd known his name before, but now, standing under his shadow with her hand nestled in the crook of his arm, she realized how well it fit him.

"Laura." He made it sound as if her name in his mouth was as sweet as candy. "Would you like to go walking again next Sunday? I could take you to see my farm."

"Yes, I would like that." And she was startled to realize how *much* she would like it. She, who had never had any kind of interest in farming, wanted to walk this man's fields with him.

How curious.

She found she couldn't wait for next Sunday.

CHAPTER FOUR

LAURA SWUNG THE KITCHEN DOOR open to reveal Catarina holding a crate of produce in her arms.

She groaned as she took it, partly because of the weight and partly because she knew what was coming.

"So how was your walk with the farmer?" Laughter threaded through her friend's voice as Laura had feared it would.

Laura turned to set the crate on the table. "It was... nice," she said to the peas within. She hated to use such an anemic word to describe their walk, but she didn't dare detail the finer emotions Marcus had inspired in her.

"Was he able to converse on anything of import, or was it all potato talk?"

"We did talk of potatoes." She smiled at the memory. "Did you know that rabbits won't eat potato plants?"

"How did you not know rabbits won't eat potato plants?"

"I'm horrid at growing things," Laura pointed out. "You know this because you're the one who takes care of my garden."

"You do have the blackest thumb of anyone I know. Speaking of black thumbs, how long do you think it took Marcus to get the dirt out from under his fingernails?" A mocking smile twitched at the corners of Catarina's mouth. "Did he even get all the dirt out?"

Annoyance bit at Laura. "His hands were quite clean." Catarina might mean all this teasing of poor Marcus to be in good fun, but Laura wasn't enjoying it.

"What *did* he do with his hands?"

"Nothing!"

"Oooh, it must have been something for your face to turn so red. I would have thought Old Farmer Marcus too much of a stick-in-the-mud for anything untoward."

"He's respectful." Lord, she sounded quite the priss, but she couldn't help it.

"You couldn't have spoken of potatoes the whole time," Catarina said. "Not even Farmer Marcus is that boring. So what did you talk about?"

"Our families."

Catarina raised her eyebrows. She knew how Laura dreaded speaking of that.

"Well, mostly his," she amended.

"Oh, the valley is simply crawling with Grieses." Catarina gave a wave to indicate how numerous they were. "Agreeable family. Dull, like Marcus."

"Marcus isn't dull. He's... quiet."

"Yes," Catarina agreed, "quietly dull." She paused to study Laura with a discomfiting intensity. "You're fond of him."

Laura felt as if her face had been washed with hot peppers. "Is that so surprising?" Defiance sharpened her words; being fond of a man was nothing to be ashamed of.

"No, it's not." Catarina nibbled at her lower lip. "But you can't truly be thinking of—"

She went quiet when Rose bustled into the kitchen.

"Oh, you brought peas," Rose exclaimed as she peered into the produce box. "They'll be lovely with the roast tonight."

"I was just asking Laura about her walk with the farmer." There wasn't even a hint of teasing in Catarina's words, but Laura's heart still sank. She had no desire to discuss Marcus in front of Rose.

Her sister-in-law began putting away the vegetables. "Oh?" she said with forced disinterest.

"You know," Catarina said to Laura, "you're the only person he's ever danced with that I've seen." She gave that searching look again. "He must be looking for a wife."

Laura's heart skittered and her breath caught while Rose paused in her unpacking, her back stiff.

"Well?" Catarina demanded. "Did he mention if he's looking for a wife?"

Laura stared at Rose's back as she swallowed hard. "The subject didn't come up."

"I suppose he wouldn't have said directly." Catarina assumed a thoughtful expression. "You have to read a man's unspoken words to see these sorts of things."

"Unspoken or not," Laura said, "he's not going to find a wife in me. So the point is moot, now isn't it?" She sent each word as a dart of warning.

Rose resumed her unpacking.

Catarina's gaze swiveled from Laura to Rose, then back again. She was considering something—how far to take this discussion of marriage with Rose listening in, no doubt—and she was doing it so intently Laura swore she could hear the hum of her thoughts.

Laura sent her own strong, unspoken thoughts to Catarina, her chest swelling with the effort to hold in her scream of *Please, stop already.*

That, or something like it, must have entered Catarina's mind, since her face went soft with pity. "Well, if you're not marrying anyone, then I suppose you won't want to know what I heard about Dr. Young."

"Dr. Young?" Laura had no idea of whom she spoke, but at least she'd given up on Marcus.

Her friend sighed in exasperation. "The doctor in Pine Ridge."

Laura rubbed at her forehead, feeling the crease of worry that seemed to grow deeper every day. Why hadn't Catarina let go of this daft idea?

"He's young," her friend went on, "like his name. He's supposedly not ugly. And he has quite the mustache." She raised her eyebrows as if this signified.

Laura sighed. "I can't say I care if a man has a mustache or not."

She rather liked Marcus's beard though. Not that a man's facial hair had been much on her mind before.

"Well, I do," Catarina said. "A clean upper lip speaks to a vanity in a man I find most unbecoming."

"And waxed and curled mustache ends do not?"

Rose chuckled. "She has a point, Catarina."

Her friend shook her head. "Do you think you might be able to overlook his mustache? Don't think on the hair on his lip; think on that fine sanatorium in Pine Ridge and him being the man in charge." Her eyebrows rose—Catarina's way of saying, *Think on his income as well.*

Laura did think on that, pondered it for the first time since the doctor had been mentioned. A doctor would be able to afford a wife and her infirm parents. If Laura took her parents to live with her and her husband, Rose would be free of her mother's constant carping.

A doctor might actually be able to help her father—perhaps not cure, but help.

For a farmer, a wife like herself—who knew nothing of farming and with two parents in tow—would be nothing but dead weight. No matter how thoughtful or caring or, yes, handsome he was.

"Mmm," Laura said in response. "I haven't yet laid eyes on this doctor, and you want me to marry him?"

"At least consider meeting him." Catarina gathered up the now-empty box and headed for the door.

As it swung shut behind her meddlesome friend, Laura looked over at Rose, who was staring into the sink. The clock ticked softly in the silence between them.

"You know I would never leave?" she said to her sister-in-law. "I would never marry and leave you alone with them."

Rose said nothing, only leaned a little farther over the sink.

"You and Frank have taken us in, all of us, and I would never repay you by abandoning you," Laura assured her. "If I marry, my parents will come with me. It will be my time to care for them. Any husband I choose must take all of us."

"I know." It was little more than a whisper. A tear fell from Rose's cheek into the wash water.

Laura crossed the room to clasp her sister-in-law's hand, clenched tight on the edge of the sink.

"Thank you," Rose said, the words heavy with her sadness. "Thank you for not abandoning me. And them."

The weight of those words—and the sentiment behind them—crashed into Laura, nearly sending her to her knees.

~~~

He was watching her, Laura knew.

Marcus was already seated when she arrived at church on Sunday. The places next to him were taken, so she slid into the pew in front of him. She was glad to be close, but also grateful she didn't have to choose whether or not to sit next to him.

As the service wore on, she realized her decision was much worse. She felt his eyes on her back the entire time, a burning that went straight through her clothes to set her skin aflame and flush her face.

She didn't hear a word of the sermon, could only hear the slow, deep drawing of his breath behind her, sensing that he was as focused on her as she was on him.

That his regard was for her and her alone made her heart stutter. An ache grew within her, an ache that deepened with every passing second, an ache that urged her to turn, to meet his gaze, to even perhaps touch him...

But she couldn't. She had to sit just so, her hands clamped in her lap, every muscle rigid as she held herself together under that shattering gaze. And when the service ended, she must calmly rise, walk with him a ways, and tell him this was their last walk.

It was the purest kind of torture, but that was exactly what she did. She sat still as a statue, rose when the service was finished, gave Marcus a merely pleasant smile as she went for the door, then met him outside.

She'd opened her mouth to begin her prepared speech when Frank appeared at her elbow and ruined it all.

"Laura, I've come to see you home for supper." Frank's voice had her jumping like a rabbit. "Mr. Gries— I'm glad I caught you. I know you and Laura were planning on taking a walk today, and I wanted to invite you to dinner. You can dine with us and then go for your walk if that suits you."

Her palm itched with the desire to box Frank's ears. How could he make this even harder for her?

"I'd like that very much," Marcus said, giving her a small smile.

Of course Marcus said yes. Why wouldn't he say yes? He thought they were courting.

Marcus's expression went from pleased to worried. She must not have kept her distress from her face.

"If that's all right with you?" he asked her.

The trouble was she wanted him to come to dinner. She wanted to put her hand in the crook of his elbow, feel his body brush against hers as they walked to the store, and then sit him in a place of pride at her family's table. She wanted her father to talk with him of male things, like politics, and to have her mother beam at her for bringing home such a nice young man.

She wanted her family to be like others.

"Of course," she said. "We would love to have you for Sunday dinner." She summoned a weak smile for him, but the question lingering in his eyes told her he wasn't entirely convinced.

Dinner would be a tense, stilted affair, far different from what Marcus would be expecting. Her father would sit, silent and expressionless like always, while her mother's discontent would make every bite bitter.

Perhaps she wouldn't have to tell him she couldn't walk with him any longer; one dinner with her family ought to change his mind.

Marcus and Frank kept up a steady conversation on all the latest happenings, neither inviting her to join in. Which was fine with her; she was too wound up with anxious apprehension to chat comfortably.

But Marcus kept sneaking glances at her as if sensing she was upset rather than shy.

The sight of the mercantile was almost unwelcome. Oh, to have avoided this from the very beginning! If only her brother had kept his mouth shut.

"We're home and we have guests," Frank called out in Dutch when they came through the door. "My mother can't speak English," he explained to Marcus. "You don't speak Dutch by any chance?"

"No, but I know German."

She turned to him in astonishment. "You speak German?"

His smile was gently teasing. "I'm a man of many hidden talents. Do your parents speak German?"

The hope flooding through her was dangerous, but she let it come anyway. "They do."

"I should have tried that last Sunday, hmm?"

"No, it was my fault," she insisted. "I should have thought of it—"

"Don't keep Marcus waiting in the hallway, Laura," Frank broke in. "Take him into the parlor to meet everyone."

The introductions went well. Her father was able to rise and shake Marcus's hand with only minimal effort, and her mother, albeit with a sour cast to her mouth, answered him in German with reasonable civility. Rose's face was tight, but otherwise her manner was entirely welcoming.

Marcus made certain to speak with everyone, looking as though he were meant to fit in with this family.

The sight would have broken her heart if she let it.

But at the dinner table, things began to unravel.

It began well, with Marcus taking the seat to her left while Rose and her mother sat across from them. Marcus dug into the roast chicken with pleasure, complimenting Rose on her cooking as he did so.

That, of course, set her mother off on her second-favorite complaint: Rose's cooking.

"I don't see how any of you can eat this," she said peevishly. "It certainly interferes with my digestion. And I don't see why Rose can't make more of an effort to make palatable food. It's not difficult to cook properly, but Rose can't seem to master it."

Laura stared at her mother, ice cracking along her spine. Rose set her fork down and lowered her head.

Marcus was blinking as if he couldn't quite believe what he'd heard. No doubt in his family, people weren't denigrated in such a fashion.

"Mother, Rose's cooking is excellent. Please just eat." The weariness in Frank's voice caught at Laura. It must be exhausting, forever caught between his wife and his mother.

She was exhausted from witnessing it day in and day out.

"I understand you're a farmer?" Frank tried to steer the conversation to something innocuous.

"Hard work, farming." Every head at the table turned toward her father.

"Yes, sir, it is," Marcus said, clearly relieved at the change in subject, "but I imagine keeping a store is hard work in its own way."

"Get to stay inside when it's too hot or too cold."

Marcus smiled. "But you also have to stay inside when the weather's fine."

Her father pulled his face into his version of a smile. "Family of farmers?"

"Yes, my father is a farmer, my four brothers are farmers, and my five sisters married farmers," he said proudly.

With that kind of lineage, he couldn't have been anything but a farmer, Laura supposed.

"So many children," her mother said wistfully. "Your parents must have quite a few grandchildren." She sent a speaking look to Rose.

Marcus's smile dimmed a bit, no doubt sensing the undercurrents he had waded into. "Yes, they do. Eleven, as a matter of fact."

Her mother's sigh was dramatic. "We, unfortunately, have none. With Mr. Kemper's and my illnesses, grandchildren would have been such a comfort, but..."

The silence was stunned and still. Horrified.

"I am sorry to hear that you and Mr. Kemper aren't well," Marcus said with utmost sincerity. His tone was a dart straight to her heart.

Gripping her fork tightly enough to cut into her palm, Laura addressed her mother. "Please, let's talk of something else. Mr. Gries came here for good company, not to hear our woes."

"Oh, no, we can talk of anything your mother likes—"

"No!" The word was too vehement, but she had to stop him.

"You know, all week Laura's been talking of how you grow potatoes," Frank said with false joviality. "Perhaps after dinner you could take her to see your farm so she can see it herself."

Marcus's ears and nose went red, and Laura felt an answering flush in her own face. No doubt Frank thought he was being kind in encouraging this budding romance.

She thought she might choke on it.

She also wanted to grab it with both hands.

Her father decided for them. "Go see the farm." He pulled that smile again, the one that no longer reached his eyes. "See the potatoes."

"I'll do the washing up," Rose offered, "so you can leave as soon as you're done with supper." She disappeared into the kitchen before Laura could read her expression, but her voice had been thick with emotion.

With her entire family beaming at her—except for her mother and Rose—Laura's fate was sealed.

She'd go out, see the farm Marcus so loved, and then break both their hearts.

CHAPTER FIVE

DINNER HAD NOT QUITE BEEN what Marcus was expecting.

He'd known there must be some reason why Mr. and Mrs. Kemper were never seen in public, and after seeing Mr. Kemper's condition, Marcus understood. As for Mrs. Kemper, the only sickness she seemed to have was a deep bitterness toward her daughter-in-law.

Truth be told, he could understand it some. It had to be terrible to watch the person you loved sink into the kind of illness Mr. Kemper had. It'd turn even the happiest person unpleasant at times. Although, if he had to guess, Mrs. Kemper hadn't been the happiest person to begin with.

Even now, Laura was in his favorite spot, by his side, her arm tucked in his as they walked out to his farm. He'd been waiting for this moment all week, and when he saw her come into church today he'd thought his heart might beat right out of his chest.

She didn't seem entirely happy though. *He* was about to burst with pride at the thought of showing her all his hard work, even as he worried at her subdued mien.

"Your folks are very nice," he offered.

"I'm sorry." It was only just above a whisper. "They didn't used to be like that."

He almost feigned incomprehension for a moment before deciding against it. There should be no deceit between them.

"It looks like it's hard for your father to get around anymore," he said carefully. "Your mother said she was sick too?"

Laura's bright head came up at that. "My mother's not ill; she's simply... angry."

Exactly what he'd thought. "Watching a loved one go through what your father is will do that to a person."

"You see now why they never go out?"

"Well, I can see why it might be difficult for your father, but—" He stopped, unsure if he should cross that line.

"But what?"

He took a breath and decided to be daring. "It seems to me that your mother might be more content if she got out some." The tension rising in her arm fed into his entire body.

"She thinks that since he's ill," Laura said with some heat, "she needs to be at his side always. No matter that she's no real help to him. And even if she would go out, she's never learned English, so she couldn't visit with anyone anyway."

The unhappiness in her voice cut him right to the bone. He loved her and wanted nothing more than for her to be happy. Wanted to be the instrument of her happiness, if he could. She *deserved* to be happy.

And then everything became clear to him.

He'd marry her.

He'd marry her and take her away from this sadness. He saw it as clearly as he would a field to be planted, how to put the irrigation, where to put the rows, the best drainage.

He'd get a ring, propose next week, and in a month or so, they could set up house.

And then she would be happy.

He puffed his chest out at his own cleverness. Some might say he was moving too fast, but he'd known for a while he wanted Laura as his wife. He'd only needed to work up the courage to approach her. But now that he had, there was no sense in waiting, especially seeing how unhappy she was at home.

He couldn't wait to show her the farm, show her all the work he'd done, show her it could be a happy home for the both of them. But best not to say anything until he saw how she reacted. A city-raised lady might take some convincing to become a farm wife.

Her smile when they came in sight of the farm proved that she would need no convincing at all.

"You cleared all this yourself? And planted it?" The awe in her voice as she surveyed his field made him feel like a giant.

"Yes. I cleared out the red shank, the sagebrush, and the chamisal. It took several months to do this field, and I've still got other acres I'm planning on clearing once the irrigation is ready."

"You get your water from there?" She pointed to the pond on the eastern edge of his land.

"I do, but if I want to irrigate every acre, I'll need more water than that." He hesitated. Suppose she found all this boring? A farmer could talk about irrigation all day, but most folks could only take a few seconds of it.

She was looking out at the pond, her face a portrait in the most serious concentration. "How will you get more water then?"

She *did* want to talk about it. "I have an idea," he said. "For digging deeper wells. But I need to buy the equipment to test it."

He needed a few good harvests to save up the money first. Knowing a farmer's luck, he'd probably have those wells in ten years.

She stared rather fiercely at the pond, and he could almost hear the gears cranking in her head. "Farming is hard work," she finally said, "but you obviously have a plan."

"Well, plans or no, I'm still at the mercy of the weather," he admitted. "One late frost and this crop right here could disappear."

"And then what?" She never looked away from the pond, but he felt her focus on his answer.

Perhaps too much focus for someone who knew nothing of farming.

"If there's time, plant again. Otherwise, there's always next spring."

"But there's no money coming in from a crop that year." Harsh. Almost accusing.

"No. But we wouldn't starve," he said hastily.

She said nothing, merely kept staring at the pond, the weight of her silence pressing hard against his chest. Her fists rhythmically clenched and unclenched, no doubt in time to the thoughts twisting in her head, but what those might be, he could not guess at.

Finally, she turned to look at him. Her eyes had gone smoky, her expression enigmatic. "Wouldn't we?" she asked, the words opaque.

She began to walk toward his house.

He felt that something had just gone horribly, terribly wrong. But for the life of him, he couldn't figure how it had happened in a conversation about irrigation.

~~~

THE WORST WAS THAT SHE could see it.

Laura could see herself standing next to Marcus, looking over the leafy potato plants in the fields they'd cleared, both of them standing together on their farm. She could even hear their children in the background.

She fisted her hands into her skirts, her legs pumping as she made for the house. It was the height of rudeness to simply turn from him as she had, but her heart couldn't take it anymore, seeing that dream right in front of her and knowing it would never be.

And it couldn't be. He'd said himself farming was hard work. Hard work, with no guarantee of success. If it were only herself to think of, she'd happily starve with him. But life didn't work like that. You didn't come into this world without attachments, without obligations. You had to honor those things or you'd be lost.

She felt lost right now.

His heavy tread from behind reached her as she set her foot on the front-porch step.

"Is everything all right?" he asked. "Laura, did I say something wrong?"

She couldn't hurt him, even as she wanted to lash out at the impotence of her situation.

She summoned a smile as she turned to him. "Nothing. I only needed to come out of the sun." The lie tasted bitter, but the truth would be worse.

He said nothing but kept frowning at her with concern. Why did he have to be so considerate? Why did he have to lavish her with all this kindness? He could have picked any other girl at that dance.

Yet she was still happy he'd picked her.

"You can go inside, look around some if you'd like." He gestured to the front door. "I'll wait out here for you."

Of course, he wouldn't go in with her, being such a gentleman. It would be unseemly for them to be alone together in his house.

She looked at the front door as a wave of curiosity hit hard enough to make her skin tingle. What would his house look like? She had to know, now that he'd offered.

She opened the door slowly, wanting to prolong the moment of revelation. After all, she'd never see his house again after today, and she wanted to learn it as best she could. Because his house would tell her about him, and she was hungry for the details.

It was exactly as she had expected and still a complete surprise. The little farmhouse was taken up mostly by a main room attached to a kitchen, with two closed doors she supposed were bedrooms. The house was smaller than the rooms behind the mercantile, yet the light streaming through the curtained windows made it seem more expansive.

Best of all, it was neat as a pin. For a bachelor's house, that was surprising, but given how graceful, how careful Marcus was, she should have known that it would be so well kept. Just like his fields. This was the home of a man who took loving care of the things that were precious to him.

Perhaps she might have been one of those things were her situation different.

She took one last turn, committing as much as she could to memory, then stepped out onto the porch.

He was waiting where she'd left him, at the top of the steps. The worry line between his eyebrows called for her fingers to smooth it away. She pinched at the neckline of her dress instead.

"You have quite the cozy home," she said. "Very tidy, even for a bachelor."

That lovely, warm smile of his lit his face. "Well, I do like things to be squared away. It's small, I know—"

"No," she said, unable to bear him belittling that lovely house. "You ought to be very proud of it. And you obviously are."

He simply stared at her for a moment as if he was searching for something to say. Or searching for the courage to say it.

"I suppose we'd best be heading back now." He turned and walked down the porch steps, but she knew that wasn't what he'd wanted to say.

She went after him. "What—?"

He turned suddenly, and she landed right into his chest. His arms wrapped around her, lifting her up as he had at the dance, protecting her from falling.

"Are you all right?" His arms around her were tight, tighter than they'd been at the dance.

She looked up into those brown eyes of his, her neck craning and craning. A spark leaped between them, a spark that erased all memory of what he'd been asking.

"Hmm?" she asked dazedly.

But he hadn't heard her, or if he had, he'd forgotten, because his head was now lowering, his lips perilously close to hers. She let her eyes flutter closed, his nearness making it impossible for her to sense anything except his large, hard body against hers, his breath fanning across her face.

Then his lips touched hers.

It was more a brushing of lips than a proper kiss, yet there was a tentative question behind it. She pressed her lips more firmly against his, answering him with a yes.

As the kiss grew stronger, deeper, still he held back, the tension in the muscles under her hands a testament to that. He tasted every corner of her mouth, reverently kissing each inch before gently nipping at her bottom lip, his beard tickling her chin.

She sighed with pleasure, opening to invite him to explore even more deeply. At the first taste of his tongue, a lightning strike of sensation moved through her, equal parts surprise and desire. He must have sensed it too, because he began to pull away.

She clutched at him in protest, pressing herself against the hard plane of him. He groaned against her mouth at the friction and threaded one hand through her hair, pulling loose her hairpins in his quest to anchor her mouth more firmly under his.

His tongue stabbed even deeper now, thrusting and retreating in a rhythm that made her breasts tingle and ignited a slow ache deep in her belly. Shamelessly, she wanted to rub herself over every inch of him, to feel the hardness of him on every part of her.

His hands went low, wrapping around her bottom and lifting her clear off her feet. She threaded her arms around his neck, clinging as hard as she could while never letting their mouths part for even a second. At the drag of her body across his, her hips gave a little buck, against her will, as if the ache he'd set off now controlled her body.

With that, that little roll of her hips that she'd never meant to make, she came back to herself.

She was kissing a man in broad daylight. More than kissing—he was lifting her off the ground, and she was rubbing her body against his.

She tore her mouth away from his, shame burning her from her head to her toes. She had come here meaning to tell him that she couldn't go walking with him anymore, and instead she was kissing him. This was not herself; this was not how she behaved.

As he lowered her back to the ground, she kept her eyes firmly down. Goodness only knew what he thought of her after that little display. She took several quick steps back when her feet hit solid ground, both her and Marcus breathing heavily into the perfumed air of spring.

"I'm sorry," he said. The regret in his voice was a lash to her smarting conscience.

"I'm the one who needs to apologize," she said quietly. "I don't know what you must think of me now." Shame settled like a leaden weight on her neck, forcing her head to droop.

"I think that you're the kindest, most beautiful—" He stopped, sighed. "Can't you even bear to look at me?"

She slowly raised her head, knowing she was a coward for fearing to meet his eyes. She'd done this to herself, and now she must answer for it.

The hurt written on his face was even worse than the disgust she'd feared.

"I swear," he said, "I swear, I am so sorry, I won't do that again, only don't—"

The pleading in his voice tore at her. "Please. Stop. I acted like a hussy."

"You could never act like a hussy. You're too much the lady."

"And you're too much the gentleman."

His smile was a rueful quirk. "A gentleman shouldn't have done what I just did."

And a lady shouldn't have done what she'd just done. "We mustn't do that again."

No matter how much she had enjoyed it, no matter how badly it hurt to know that would be the one and only kiss they would share, she had to keep herself safe. Any more kisses like that, and she'd be liable to forget her duty to herself and her family.

He looked at her intently, again with that expression that said he was gathering his courage. It was the same expression he'd worn before he'd asked her to dance. Except this time he said, "I suppose we really should be getting back now."

Once again, she knew it wasn't what he'd truly wanted to say.

CHAPTER SIX

MARCUS PEERED INTO THE MERCANTILE, searching the dim corners for any signs of life, ready to bolt at a moment's notice.

Only Frank was inside. Perhaps it was safe to enter.

He moved cautiously inside, still searching for any hidden customers.

"Marcus! How are you today?" Frank's smile was dangerously close to a smirk. The shopkeeper must have some idea of why he was here, which would make it that much harder to get out his request.

He had to swallow hard before he could trust his voice. "I'm doing well. How are you?"

"Can't complain. Laura's fine too." Did Frank... *wink* at him?

"That's... that's good to hear."

"What can I help you with?"

His tongue felt thick in his mouth. He'd practiced exactly what he would say, but here before Frank all his carefully memorized words disappeared.

Lord, what to say? What to say?

Frank's smile shifted from teasing to sympathetic. "Laura likes you quite a bit," he said with perhaps more kindness than he needed to.

Marcus's chest lightened, his tongue coming unstuck. "Does she? I—"

He couldn't say he liked her as well. What he felt was much too strong for *like*. *Like* didn't take possession of a man, didn't stitch its way into his very soul. But he couldn't admit that to Frank.

He also couldn't admit he'd kissed the man's sister and it had been wondrous. He'd been having dreams about her that no man should have about any lady, even if he did intend to take her to wife.

Instead, he cleared his throat and said something appropriately tepid. "She's a fine young lady."

"She is indeed," Frank agreed. "She deserves a man who'll treat her right, who'll care for her and keep her safe."

That caught Marcus up short. Had he treated her as he should? She'd been terribly subdued on the walk back to the mercantile, disappearing without even a "by your leave," but he'd attributed that to her natural modesty. Had her silence been one of revulsion instead?

And then there had been her strange silence by the pond, followed by that odd "Wouldn't we," said so coldly, so harshly, he would not have thought it was her voice if he hadn't seen her speak the words. Perhaps she didn't want to farm, didn't believe he could—

No. He set his jaw and commanded his nerve not to fail. He had asked her to dance, and she had said yes. He had asked her to walk with him, and she had said yes. Now he had to summon the courage to ask her to marry him, and trust to Providence for her answer.

"I understand," he said. "She deserves only the best." He hoped Frank understood his unspoken assurance that, as her husband, he would ensure she received only the best.

Frank nodded, but speculation sparked in his eye. "Farming's a hard life."

"It is, but I come from a long line of farmers, and I've got big plans for my place." If they were worried about him being a farmer—well, he'd show them that if there was anything he knew, it was farming.

"Laura told me a little about it. Still a long way off though, isn't it?"

"It's better to save up and buy equipment outright than go into debt," Marcus argued. "A few good harvests and I'll have enough."

"Even with supporting a wife? Children?"

His nose and ears went warm at that thought, but his nerves, for once, remained steady. "Even then," he said firmly.

"Some might say a courtship of only a few weeks is too short for something as serious as marriage." Frank raised an eyebrow. "Some might say a city-raised girl won't do well as a farm wife."

"A smart city-raised lady could learn all she needed to. And when a man's known his mind for two years..."

Frank blinked. "Two years? Good God, man."

The heat of embarrassment licked at Marcus's face. How could he explain his nerves, the dread that had enveloped him when he thought of approaching her, without sounding like a coward who'd prefer to worship from afar?

But he *had* been a coward who'd worshiped from afar. He could kick himself for those lost years, knowing now what the view was like up close.

He opened and closed his mouth like a dying fish, trying to find the words. *Come on,* he urged his brain. *Come on.*

Frank would never agree to Laura marrying him if he couldn't even speak.

Come on.

But nothing came.

Frank sighed. "Mm-hmm," he said, his earlier kindness thinning. "Well, if Laura agrees, I suppose it's fine by me."

Marcus blinked, unsure if he was hearing what he thought he was hearing. "You're... you're giving your blessing?"

Frank's chuckle started in his belly before ringing out of his mouth. "Of course. You're a good man, and Laura couldn't do better." He held out his hand. "Welcome to the family."

Marcus was in a daze, his mind trying to catch up to where he was now. Had it really been that easy?

"I... Well, I'll still need to ask your father," he said, "but I figured... I thought you would be the person to ask first."

Frank might have welcomed him to the family, but Mr. Kemper's illness was still uncertain ground.

A wash of sadness came over the shopkeeper's face as his gaze went to the floor. "You were right in that," he said. "And you're right to ask my father as well." A small smile returned to his lips. "And Laura too, of course."

A tremor settled in Marcus's stomach at the thought of proposing to her. She wasn't going to carry him through if he fouled up, the way Frank had just carried him through this.

Frank clapped him on the back. "Let's go look at rings." He raised an eyebrow questioningly. "You are going to get her a ring, aren't you?"

"Of course." Marcus blinked away the fog. "I came in here for that. And to ask your permission."

He'd gotten Frank's permission. That left Mr. Kemper.

And Laura.

He followed Frank to the display box with strangely heavy feet.

~~~

As he finished up his second Sunday dinner with the Gries family, Marcus decided that while these dinners weren't exactly pleasant, it wasn't anything he couldn't manage. Not if he had Laura by his side.

Rose had invited him when she'd seen him at church, and he'd gladly accepted. Laura hadn't been in church, but he supposed that was for the best. Wasn't it bad luck to see a lady before the proposal? Or was that only the wedding?

At dinner, Laura's father hadn't said much, but Marcus hadn't been expecting him to. Frank and Rose did their best to force the conversation onward with Laura assisting them.

Mrs. Kemper, however, had decided to turn her scorn on him, almost as if she knew what he had planned for after dinner and was determined to change his mind. According to her, his German was unpolished, his table manners were an embarrassment to his mother, and apparently he still stank of the fields, even though he'd scrubbed himself in the kitchen last night.

He let all of it roll off his back. He knew what Mrs. Kemper was about; a lonely woman trapped by her husband's illness deserved his sympathy. Even if she did make it difficult to be sympathetic.

But now it was only him and Laura, walking along the road that went past Rancho Moreno and Strawberry Creek. Her hand was tucked along his side, just inches from the ring in his breast pocket.

A nervous elation filled him, almost pulling him off the ground, so different from the nervousness that made a man want to curl up in himself. He'd practiced his proposal all week, even cribbing a few lines of poetry to help him say exactly how he felt about her, only better than what he could come up with.

He had in mind a spot by the creek, where a meadow of flowers spread out beyond the bank and the water gurgled especially prettily. He'd get down on one knee, pull out the ring, and tell her how he felt. She'd smile that beautiful smile of hers, say yes, and then they would kiss.

Unless she said no.

His stomach shifted at that thought, at the vision of her soft lips popping out a firm *No*. His knees nearly gave out, his feet catching on each other.

He caught himself before he landed in the dirt, stealing a glance to see if she had seen his clumsiness. Thankfully, she was still staring straight ahead.

He had to be calm, in command. A lady wasn't going to say yes to a proposal from a man who tripped over nothing.

Had she even spoken yet? He frowned as he tried to remember. He'd been so busy reciting his proposal he wasn't sure what they'd spoken of—or if they'd spoken of anything.

She certainly wasn't speaking now, with her head down and her steps uncertain. Perhaps she was still upset about dinner, but he wasn't sure how to reassure her without making explicit reference to her mother's behavior and thereby making her feel even worse. Perhaps she felt he'd taken advantage of her last week and was worried it would happen again.

Perhaps she knew what he was about to do and was thinking of how to say no.

Panic seized him again, and he reached for his watch, needing the solidity of it in his hand and the busyness of checking the time to distract him from his nerves.

As he reached for the watch, his fingers brushed against the ring in his pocket, the endless circle of metal unyielding as he pressed against it, drawing him up short.

He could do this. His nerve needed only to be as hard, as unfailing, as the ring in his pocket. He'd spent two years waiting for the courage to ask her to dance, to walk, and when he'd finally done so, she'd said yes.

Only a fool would wait so long to ask her to marry him. And he wasn't going to be a fool, not anymore. She needed him to rescue her from her family situation, needed him to make her happy. If his nerve failed him, he was failing her.

He had only to find the perfect spot and he would do it. He swore he would.

He was all firm resolve and proud stature as he led them to his chosen spot. Then the Dragon appeared in the road.

He felt that familiar sense of helplessness sink its claws into him as she approached. He almost imagined he could see the gleam of scales in the fabric of her dress.

He commanded his nerve to stay steady, but like a cur, it slunk away, tail between its legs.

"Catarina!" The edge of Laura's voice was ragged as she called to the other girl.

His heart sank further when he realized that not only was it the Dragon but her sister Isabel as well. If there was ever a woman to strike fear into a man's heart, it was Isabel with her superior sneer and whiskey-bottle-smashing ways. A woman who could handle an ax like that was not one to cross.

"Laura! I was coming to visit you." Catarina looked him up and down with those cat's eyes. "But I see you're already out. With Mr. Gries."

Marcus didn't think he'd ever heard his name pronounced with such disdain.

"Afternoon, Miss Moreno, Miss Moreno." He tipped his hat to each in turn, stumbling a little with his numb tongue.

"Mr. Gries," Isabel said with only a hint of a nod.

He knew then that he couldn't possibly present that ring to Laura today. No man could be expected to deal with a proposal and the Dragon all in the same afternoon.

"The creek?" Catarina raised an eyebrow. "It's a fine thing we happened along then. Who knows what trouble you two would have gotten into on your own?"

Laura studied the ground while his nose and ears burned. Catarina laughed and Isabel sniffed.

"You two haven't already gotten into trouble, have you?" Catarina asked with waspish teasing. "I refuse to believe it of someone as upstanding as you are, Mr. Gries." She made *upstanding* sound as if he were near to dead.

"Mr. Gries is a perfect gentleman," Laura told her feet.

Indignation bit at him. She might have at least hinted he wasn't half so boring as Miss Moreno seemed to think.

Over the next half hour, Marcus developed an acute case of dyspepsia. Catarina kept making veiled references to how unsafe Laura would have been in his clutches while Isabel perfected her sneer. Laura didn't ignore him, exactly, but he still had the sense she was turning away from him.

He almost clicked his heels with joy once the Misses Moreno finally turned off the road to home and left Laura and him in peace. His dyspepsia left along with them.

A curious sort of lightness took hold of him when it was only the two of them. He might have called it recklessness, if he'd ever in his life been reckless.

Perhaps he could still ask her today.

Perhaps he couldn't.

His mind went back and forth on the matter, until his stomach was filled with a fluttery kind of churning, as if butterflies had turned his insides into a battlefield.

He was so worked up he didn't notice the field of lilacs until they were upon it. The flowers were great clouds of purple erupting from the greenery supporting them—the most perfect mark of spring he'd seen yet. He took a quick look up and down the road—empty as far as he could see.

It must have been a sign.

He took a deep breath. *Courage, man, courage.*

He pulled them to a stop and sank to one shaky knee. She simply stared at him, her smoke-blue eyes going wide.

He fumbled for the ring in his pocket and looked down the road, trying to summon the words he'd practiced, when he saw the steaming road apples behind her.

Lord, of all the things... He ought to scramble back up and forget this whole sorry business, at least until he could work himself up to it again.

But he was already down on one knee, and she was looking at him with those eyes...

He weighed his options. He could stand up, find a new spot, and go back down on one knee, but then he'd look a complete fool.

Or he could remain here and hope she didn't notice what was behind her.

Time to be bold. He'd simply pray that she not turn around or sniff the air too forcefully.

He set his jaw, feeling about for the ring. Where was it? He couldn't speak until he had it and the longer it took, the more likely she was to notice what was behind her.

Her delicate nose wrinkled. "Do you notice a smell?"

"No, don't notice a thing." He fisted his hand against his thigh to keep the tremors at bay, even as he sought in vain with the other for the ring.

"Are you sure? I think I smell—"

"Miss Kemper!" he said a little too loudly, startling them both. "Would you like to get married?"

She blinked and her mouth fell open.

"I mean to me. Would you like to get married to me?" What was that poem he wanted to recite? He couldn't summon a single word of it now. "I have a ring." His thick fingers finally closed on it and he held it out to her as if it were a pretty rock he'd found on the road.

She peered and frowned. It was quite possibly the fiercest frown he'd ever seen cross her face.

The butterflies resumed their battle in his stomach.

"You got this from my brother's store." She made it sound like *You* stole *this from my brother's store.*

"Well, yes," he admitted. "If you don't like it, I can get a different one." His heart began to hop about like a rabbit running for its life because she looked as if she certainly did not like it.

"My brother knew you were planning this all week, and he didn't say a thing," she said, as cold as a frostbitten morning.

Marcus felt a twinge of fear for Frank. And more than a twinge for himself.

"I think he wanted it to be a surprise?"

"No," she said flatly.

Marcus's head jerked back. No to Frank and the surprise?

Or no to him and marriage?

She was staring down at him as if he'd proposed something infinitely more dishonorable, more horrifying than marriage.

Something worse than anxiety began slithering through his gut.

"I can't marry you."

His entire chest spasmed, trapping the breath within his lungs. He stared up at her, her face hard, unyielding, looking as if she could crush the entirety of himself under her bootheel.

Which was exactly what she had just done.

"Why?" He hated how broken he sounded.

She merely looked away. "Please take me home now."

He stayed right where he was, the ring still clenched in his hand.

"Was this Catarina's idea? That you can't marry a dirt-grubber like me?" The words sounded ugly even as he said them, but he went on anyway.

She turned back to him, a crease of rage appearing between her brows. "Catarina?" she threw at him. "You think this is about her?"

What else was he meant to think? "You won't tell me what this is about."

"It's not about you."

He studied her, trying to decipher that. Everything she'd said had been in a language he'd thought completely foreign to her—cruel, callous, crushing. Yet she had said it. All of it.

She closed her eyes tightly. "Please take me home." Her voice was rough.

A single tear snuck from beneath her eyelids, traveling down the planes of her cheek to hang for a moment from her chin before disappearing into the dirt beneath their feet.

He let his hands fall back to his sides, the ring still clutched in his fist.

He had lost.

He had thought wooing her would only be a matter of working up his courage, of finally having the nerve to speak to her. Once he did that, he'd thought it would simply be a matter of courting for the appropriate time before he could propose. Then they would marry.

But this wooing business was more like farming than he'd thought. You could put in all the work you wanted, but luck would have its way with you in the end. She was about as predictable as a summer thunderstorm. You thought you were getting some much-needed rain, but instead wind and hail destroyed your crop.

He rose slowly from his ridiculous position in the dirt. It was time to call this courting season a loss.

He just wasn't sure he had it in him to try again.

"I apologize for my presumption, Miss Kemper," he stiffly. "Allow me to escort you home. I won't... *bother* you with my attentions again."

He offered his arm to her without thought, his movements those of a mechanical man who had just had his clockwork heart torn out.

CHAPTER SEVEN

THE PAIN WAS WORSE THAN Laura had thought it would be.

Marcus's face when she'd said no—that tight, pale mask of shock and hurt—refused to leave her mind's eye, appearing at unguarded moments as if summoned by an evil spirit.

Now, twenty minutes after she'd insisted he take her home, she was scrubbing at the kitchen counter with all her might, grimly enjoying the ache in her arms, the tightness in her belly.

She and Marcus had walked back in the most absolute, terrible silence. As soon as she'd seen the familiar façade of the mercantile, she'd run for its promised safety as if a pack of dogs were on her heels rather than one rejected suitor.

She'd dashed past them all—her brother, Rose, her parents, ignoring their stares, their calls to her, and fled until she reached the kitchen and could go no farther. Then she began to scrub, heedless of her Sunday best, needing only to keep her hands busy.

But his face kept appearing, despite her attempts to scour it away.

The steady, heavy thud of steps came down the hall—Frank, heading toward the kitchen. She kept her head down, eyes fixed on the counter, mouth tight.

The toes of her brother's black shoes came into her line of sight, all that she could see of him, all that she wanted to see of him. She concentrated very hard on ignoring those shoes—the shoes of a shopkeeper—in her periphery.

She didn't have to speak if she didn't want to.

The silence stretched out, broken only by the *skritch-skritch* of her rag against the counter.

"Did something happen?" Frank finally asked.

"I don't wish to talk about it, *Francis.*" She rubbed violently at a speck that had been on the counter for years.

"Did Marcus—?"

"Yes, he did," she gritted out between swipes, "and I told him no."

That Frank—her own brother, of all people—had known all along what Marcus was planning and had even encouraged him... It added the bitter taste of betrayal to the anger souring within her.

"I see."

"No, you don't," she snapped. That blasted speck wouldn't budge. "And I said I didn't wish to speak of it."

The toe of that black shoe remained right where it was, unmoving. She had a sudden vision of smashing it with her heel. And then a cloud of despair broke upon her, that she should think such unkind thoughts about her own brother.

That toe disappeared after a time, its owner moving away back down the hall, even as she kept at her scrubbing. She wished she could wash away her rage and anguish with each swipe of the rag. Wished she could wash away her entire life, really.

But the hurt, the anguish, wouldn't disappear.

After that Sunday, the Kemper household settled into an even deeper gloom. Frank continually threw her the queerest glances while Rose looked guilty, of all things. And of course her mother continued with her usual rain of complaints, never even suspecting the victory she'd won when Laura had refused her first and likely only marriage proposal.

As for herself, she felt like dough rolled too thin, with Marcus and her heart pulling one way and her family and her duty pulling the other. It would only take a tug from either side to tear her straight down the middle.

But she'd made her choice, and even though the pain tore at her day and night, she knew it was the right one. She couldn't leave her parents, and Marcus couldn't afford to feed them, especially if the harvest was poor. He might insist he could, but she knew the pain she was feeling now would be nothing to knowing that Marcus was in debt—or even worse, had lost the farm.

Knowing that she'd done the right thing didn't ease the pain, however. She found herself wanting to burst into tears whenever her mind or hands weren't occupied. In those quiet moments, she could envision the long, dark tunnel of her future before her, waiting to collapse on her like an unstable mine shaft. So she worked as if beset by a Fury, prompting her mother to complain that all her hustle and bustle was giving her a headache while Rose sent her worried looks when she thought Laura wasn't watching.

Laura ignored the both of them, just as she ignored Frank's equally concerned glances.

Her anger wouldn't let her speak rationally, so she kept quiet. After all, she was a grown woman, and she could decide if and when she wanted to marry. She didn't need them pushing her into it. They might be a little more grateful that she'd tossed away a future with Marcus to help them, rather than trying to make her feel guilty.

And guilty for what? For doing her duty? Yes, she regretted Marcus was hurt, but that was life. If she had to spend the rest of hers watching her father decline and her mother decline right along with him, Marcus could withstand a little heartache.

And Marcus. What had he been thinking, proposing so precipitously? As if dancing with her and walking with her meant she was his for the asking? She wasn't some trinket in her brother's store, to be taken from the shelf when she was required. She was a creature with free will, and she could say no if she chose.

And she chose to say no. So that was that.

Catarina had been her sole comfort when she'd visited. She'd taken a long look at Laura's face but said not a thing of import—only keeping up a steady stream of chatter while Laura wordlessly sniffled. Every so often her friend would reach over and pat her hand, which had been immensely soothing. Catarina was the only one who had given her permission simply to *feel.*

As they were hugging good-bye, her friend had whispered, "A doctor never knows a lack of meat at his table." Laura had stilled at that while the other girl continued, "You might not be able to marry Marcus, but you could escape this. You could still be happy."

Laura had said nothing, merely watched with damp eyes as her friend left.

The week was a haze of anger, bitterness, and misery as she kept her mouth shut tight and her hands busy so she didn't strike out in her sorrow at those nearest to her.

Then something extraordinary happened. A few small, extraordinary somethings.

~~~

Marcus spent Monday brooding.

He had thought Laura a lady in a tower, pining for rescue, anticipating the day a brave knight would release her from her confinement.

But in the stories the lady in the tower never said no to the knight.

Not that Marcus was any kind of brave knight; he was only a thickheaded potato farmer, as the events of yesterday had proven.

He sat in his little house, surrounded by his fields, and rethought the disastrous proposal again and again, the way you'd push on an aching tooth, hoping that this time the pain would be less, that it had begun to heal.

But each time he remembered, he squeezed a little more pain out—the horror on her face, the flat, final way she'd said no. You knew a proposal was terrible when horse droppings were the least bad aspect of it.

He also had some very uncharitable thoughts about the Moreno sisters.

When reflecting on that nightmare of a proposal lost its glitter, he began to brood on everything else. Everything Laura had said or done. When she had been unhappiest with him. What he might have done to cause that unhappiness.

He knew that speaking of her parents made her unhappy; that hadn't taken too much figuring.

But her reaction when he'd talked about the weather and the possibility of the crop failing niggled at him. She'd seemed almost mercenary in that moment, and he'd have never taken her as someone who cared so much about money. If she wanted to be a rich man's wife, there were plenty of men she could have pursued.

But she'd never pursued any man that he'd seen.

Marcus kept hearing her say those words, "Wouldn't we?" and watching her turn from him, her body stretched too tight, the moment unspooling again and again in his mind as he searched it for meaning.

That *we* had been too heavy, with the weight of more than two people behind it. What could she have meant by it? Was she worried they wouldn't be able to feed their children? Of course he would do everything and anything to keep their children fed—that was the natural duty of a parent.

She'd never pursued any man that he'd seen.

He groaned and dropped his head into his hands, tugging his hair in punishment for his stupidity.

Her parents.

She didn't want to leave her parents, and she thought he couldn't afford to support them all. It explained everything—her worries about the crops, her comment that it wasn't about him, even her acceptance of his invitations.

She liked him, she might even want to marry him, but she couldn't leave her parents and she couldn't take them with her.

He, being a right idiot, had thought he would be rescuing her from them. She didn't want rescuing from her own family; she needed her entire family to be rescued.

Lord, what a fool he'd been! Shoving that ring in her face without even properly speaking with her. He'd convinced himself that since she'd said yes to a dance and a walk, she had to say yes to a marriage.

But a walk and a dance were nothing. Now marriage... marriage was everything.

She was correct about not being able to support her *and* her parents. He had barely a third of his land cleared for planting. And there was still the problem of irrigating it. Give him a few good years and he could support them all, but not yet.

He admired her for her devotion her parents. It made him love her even more—although it was preventing him from marrying her.

If he took her away from her family, his life might be enriched, but the lives of those left behind would be poorer.

He tapped his fingers against the wooden arm of the chair, his brows pulling toward each other.

So what to do about it?

She was unhappy, that was for certain. The entire Kemper house was unhappy; he'd seen that for himself. Laura might not wish to marry him, but surely there was something he could do to make her happier? He'd rather she be happy and out of his reach than in his arms and miserable.

He thought on it all day Tuesday.

He went to see some people about it on Wednesday.

CHAPTER EIGHT

LAURA HAD ALWAYS LIKED JAMES Harper, so her smile when he walked in the store on Thursday was her most genuine one all week.

"How are you, Mr. Harper?"

The older man's smile was dazzling in his dark face. "Quite well, Miss Kemper. How's your family doing?"

"They're all well," she said with sincere politeness, although the words themselves were false. "What can I help you with today?"

He peered into a barrel of crackers. "I thought I might visit with your pa for a bit."

She faltered for a moment. "My father? He—" She scrambled for the right words. "His English is... imperfect." Which was the smallest reason why he couldn't visit, but it would do.

Mr. Harper moved to the checkerboard set up in a corner of the shop. "You don't need to speak much to play checkers," he said. "The rules are the same everywhere, right?"

"I... I suppose so."

Her father, in the front of the store? He would never agree to being so exposed to everyone's view.

And what would her mother say?

Frank came in from the back. "Morning, Mr. Harper. If you want to play checkers, I'm sure Mr. Whitman will be along soon."

"Actually, I thought I'd play with your pa."

A look passed between the two men, one Laura couldn't decipher.

"I can see if he's here," Frank said.

Their father never went anywhere. Where else would he be?

"I appreciate it," Mr. Harper said. "The boys don't want me underfoot anymore, so I need to find other folks to bother."

"Mr. Harper, I don't think your boys want you to leave," Laura said. "I hope they never said any such thing."

His smile was gently teasing. "Oh, not in so many words, but a man knows when his children don't need his advice anymore."

Frank came back, leading their father. His shuffling steps were less hesitant than usual—today was one of his good days.

Mr. Harper grasped her father's hand and shook it for the both of them.

"Pleased to see you, Mr. Kemper. Thought you might want to take pity on me and play some checkers this morning."

Her father nodded his agreement, the movement stiff and forced, but decisive for all that.

To Laura's amazement, they played game after game that morning, barely a word passing between the two. But both were smiling when Mr. Harper took his leave.

The strange happenings didn't end there. Mrs. Crivelli came that afternoon to sit with her mother and sew. Laura tried to explain that her mother didn't speak English but didn't get far.

"Oh, I speak some Dutch," Mrs. Crivelli said as she waved Laura off. "I learned a bit when I was a girl. I think we'll get by fine."

And they had. Both women had complained about the young people of today and their lack of grandchildren, although Mrs. Crivelli made them seem more like jests rather than complaints.

Before she left, Mrs. Crivelli got a promise from Mrs. Kemper that she would see her in church on Sunday so they could continue their conversation.

Laura was all astonishment as she let Mrs. Crivelli out the door while the older lady flashed a knowing smile at her.

Her mother said not one rude word to Rose the entire day.

People kept visiting. Mr. Harper was there without fail every morning, seemingly content to while away his time by playing checkers in absolute silence. Mrs.

Whitman and Mrs. Larsen each came to visit her mother on separate occasions. Although they had to rely on Laura to translate, her mother never complained about it—she was too busy gossiping about all the town residents she had never yet met.

Laura even found herself receiving a few visitors. Luke Crivelli came into the store on Thursday, chatted with her for a long while, and left without buying a thing. On Friday, Bill Whitman came by the store and asked if she would like to take a drive the next day. She said no as politely as she could, bewildered by the sudden attention after two years of being in Catarina's shade.

It seemed as if a signal had gone out amongst the young men of Cabrillo that Miss Laura Kemper was accepting suitors.

But as nice as it had been, none of the visitors was the one she truly wanted to see.

So while the entire mood of the Kemper household lightened over that week, Laura found herself sinking deeper, knowing that no matter how things improved, she'd never get her happy ending.

~~~

That Saturday was the warmest day of spring so far. Laura was out tending her little garden, although she feared that with her inexperience she was doing more harm than good. After an hour, she figured she'd done enough damage to those innocent plants and headed indoors.

Only to find Catarina and an unfamiliar man in the parlor, taking tea with Rose.

"Laura!" Catarina called with a gaiety that had fooled many a man before.

Laura was having quite the time puzzling out this little tableau. What was this strange man doing in her parlor?

"Catarina, how lovely to see you." She raised her eyebrows in question before turning to the stranger in her father's chair.

"Laura, this is Dr. Young. Dr. Young, this is Miss Laura Kemper, whom I was telling you all about."

Laura nearly laughed as she settled into a chair. So Catarina had actually spirited the infamous Dr. Young into Cabrillo. Her friend's description of him had been correct—he was young and not ugly. The best word to fit him would be *moderate*. A man of moderate height, moderate handsomeness and, no doubt, moderate opinions. A man of moderate passions.

And the lady he chose for a wife would most certainly be the epitome of moderation—in all things. Laura supposed that described her as well as anything.

"Dr. Young, what a pleasure to meet you," she said, remembering her manners. "Catarina tells me that you work in the sanatorium in Pine Ridge. What brings you all this way to Cabrillo?"

His answering smile was pleasant enough, but it didn't send her heart to skittering. Not like Marcus's.

"We occasionally take the patients for excursions outside Pine Ridge—the air is so healthful for the lungs, you see—and I happened to meet Miss Moreno on one such excursion last week. When she invited me to visit your charming little town, I could not resist." The smile he sent to Catarina was a familiar one, full of dazzle and infatuation, the smile that every young man in town had given her at some point.

Except for Marcus.

Catarina resembled a great, satisfied cat, one that had just deposited a fat gopher on the step for everyone's admiration. But poor Dr. Young was no gopher. Only another silly man caught up in the siren's net.

"I knew the two of you would get along famously," Catarina said.

As Catarina turned back to Laura, the doctor's face fell and Laura could see the exact moment he realized that the net set for him was not to be pulled in by Miss Moreno.

The doctor studied Laura with a new kind of intention then.

She knew what he must be seeing. Hair the color of a sunbaked road, eyes too dark to be blue but too light to be gray, and a nose that sailed right past pert and landed squarely on snub.

Certainly nothing that could be compared with the incomparable Miss Moreno.

His smile was that of a man offered a turnip when he wanted a peach. "I am certain Miss Kemper and I will find some things of common interest." He turned to Catarina, and the smile returned to dazzling. "But tell me, Miss Moreno, when can we expect to see you in Pine Ridge?"

Catarina gave her tinkling laugh. "Oh, perhaps soon. Miss Kemper, I'm sure, would adore Pine Ridge. All those… pine trees."

Laura covered her mouth to keep her laughter from bubbling out. As if Cabrillo didn't have an abundance of pines!

"Tell me, Dr. Young," said Rose from her rocker, never looking up from her knitting, "do you treat patients for creeping paralysis in your sanatorium?"

The doctor's tongue darted out to wet his lips. "Well, the mountain air, you see—"

"Yes, yes," Rose interrupted, "you've mentioned the mountain air as a cure, but I wasn't speaking of consumption. I was speaking of creeping paralysis."

The doctor took a sip of tea. "No, we don't treat creeping paralysis. There is no cure." His voice was cool, reflecting his pique that he had been thwarted in his boosterism. "Do you have a family member with this affliction?"

Rose simply kept on with her knitting, so Laura answered instead. "My father."

His nod was sympathetic and dismissive all at once. "I am sorry." He turned back to Catarina, the true object of his interest, and once again Laura found herself in her usual place. The object of pity, hidden in Catarina's shadow.

Freed from his examination, she could study him at leisure. Could she really pursue this man and dispassionately lure him into marriage? She forced herself to think on it, to imagine herself and her parents surrounded by the fine furnishings of the sanatorium—no charity patients there—and herself facing this man across the supper table each night.

No, she didn't think she could. She had no doubt that he was a good man. Perhaps even a fine one, spending his days curing the sick as he did, but he was not the man for her.

"Every Saturday, the Pine Ridge Resort has a dance in their main ballroom," he was saying. "Everyone is invited, and I'm sure that you—both of you," he said with a nod in Laura's direction, "would enjoy it immensely."

She smiled and nodded in return, feeling a bit sorry for the poor man. He had no doubt thought he'd be enjoying Catarina's attention this fine afternoon, and instead she was trying to foist him onto Laura. It was a long way to come for such a disappointment.

"That sounds quite lovely," Laura said, "but I'm afraid I could not leave my parents for so long." She looked to Rose to provide confirmation of her excuse, but her sister-in-law's gaze was firmly on her knitting, a frown twisting her mouth.

"We have barn dances here in Cabrillo," Catarina offered. "You would certainly enjoy one."

The doctor's mouth pinched in a moue of distaste before he could school himself back to politeness.

Indignation buzzed in Laura. Cabrillo was her home, and if he would turn his nose up at an entertainment with her friends and neighbors for a dance filled with tourists you would never see again…

Catarina had caught the look as well, and without even knowing it, the doctor had just snuffed any hopes he might have had of winning over the lovely Miss Moreno. Snubbing Cabrillo was the quickest way to losing her affections.

"Or perhaps not," Catarina said coolly to him. "Perhaps that would be too far for you to travel."

He leaned back and swallowed, no doubt realizing his mistake. "With my work in the sanatorium, it is best that I not travel too far. In fact," he said, rising and going for his hat, "I must be getting back now. Miss Moreno,

Miss Kemper, Mrs. Kemper, it was a pleasure to meet you all."

As Laura watched his retreating back, she breathed a sigh of relief. Spending the rest of her life alone would certainly be better than settling for that.

CHAPTER NINE

LAURA CAREFULLY ARRANGED HER SKIRTS as she sat down in the church pew, determined to look her best in case she happened to see Marcus.

It was the kind of vanity that she'd always found ridiculous in Catarina but couldn't seem to help in this case.

It certainly didn't help that everyone was staring at them. Because for the first time ever, the entire Kemper family was in church, all squeezed together in a row.

There had been some doubt as to whether it would happen since her father was quite weak today, but her mother insisted. It seemed that the lure of more gossip was stronger than the shame of exposing her husband for all the town to gawk at.

Laura forced herself to take a deep breath and pinched the back of her hand as the urge to pluck at her neckline rose in her. Everyone *would* look, but she wouldn't give them the pleasure of knowing it affected her.

One by one, the families of the town filed in, each stopping to greet them before heading to their own pews.

Laura held herself rigid, waiting for all those heads to swivel back for one last stare at her father.

They never did.

Heads bent together to whisper, or stared straight ahead, or turned to greet another newcomer, but none turned back to stare at them.

A sense of foolishness trickled down her throat. What had she been thinking, assuming the town was so rude, so starved for entertainment, that they'd gape at them like animals in a cage? Everyone had their own concerns, their own worries, and no one seemed to want to bother about theirs.

She stared down at her hands, studying the whiteness of her knuckles as she clenched them against each other. They had immured themselves in the back of the store, in those dark, small rooms, for this? For all those reasons that had proved to be as insubstantial as the wind?

Her parents couldn't speak English? Well then, people spoke Dutch. Or German. Or asked Laura to translate. Such a simple solution.

Her father's illness made his face blank and his motions difficult? Well, look at Mr. Larsen, who'd lost an arm, or Old Mr. Whitman, who'd had an apoplexy. They were here in church today, and everyone greeted them as warmly as they did any able-bodied person.

She had been so foolish. Her parents had been ready to sink into bitterness and despair, and she'd been prepared to be pulled down with them without even a fight.

With all her heart, she wished Marcus were here. She didn't know how she'd tell him what she'd realized, didn't know if she could put into words the mix of shame and hope that was now swirling within her, but she wanted the chance to try.

The preacher stood, calling the service to attention.

Marcus was nowhere in sight.

He wasn't coming.

She swallowed hard and tried to concentrate on the preacher's words. She was trying so hard she ignored the rustling in the pew in front of them as everyone shifted to make way for a latecomer. A space opened right in front of her, which was then filled by a man's broad back.

A back that she knew very well.

She stared, wondering if he could feel her gaze on him, as she had felt his on her before. Did her look heat his skin the way he'd heated hers? She ran her gaze up and down his back, imagining her hand tracing that hard expanse, feeling the muscle gather and bunch beneath her fingertips.

It was wrong to be so wicked in church, but she couldn't help it.

She wondered if he could feel her breath against the back of his neck, little stirrings barely teasing the dark brown curls that touched his collar. Could he hear the ragged edges of it, knowing that the air slipped and pulled along the column of her throat because she was thinking of his lips against hers, his hands cupping her body?

"Laura, are you all right? Your breathing is... queer."

Rose's whisper made her heart stop.

"I'm fine." It was the barest of squeaks.

Rose frowned but said no more. Laura's entire body burned, from her toes to the ends of her hair. She wouldn't be surprised if her dress ignited from the embarrassed heat coming off her.

But in spite of the flames running under her skin, she couldn't look away. The curl of his soft hair, the smooth column of his neck with its sun-browned skin, and the stretch of his coat against those strong shoulders all forced her to look.

She was helpless against it. Against him.

Thankfully, the service ended before she could melt completely into the floor. But she did stagger a bit when Marcus finally turned and sent her a slow, sweet smile. A smile that said he knew exactly what she'd been up to.

She had to look away before she fell completely and busied herself with helping her mother out the door.

And, of course, he followed.

As she'd hoped he would.

~~~

Marcus's skin was still tingling when he caught up with Laura outside. Those smoky eyes of hers had speared him straight through before she'd turned away to help her mother.

The fact that they'd shown up to church meant that his plan was working, but he wasn't sure if it was working well enough yet. If he could convince her to walk with him today, he'd take that final step. It might kill him to do it, but if losing the thing he loved second best in this world gained him the thing he loved best, he would do it.

"Miss Kemper?"

The grace of her turn made the breath catch in his lungs. He couldn't wait to teach her to dance. Properly.

"Mr. Gries." The rasp of her voice sent shivers along his nerves. Her cheeks were delightfully pink, but her eyes met his directly.

"How are you this fine day, Miss Kemper?"

"Quite well, Mr. Gries. And you?"

"I can't complain. Did you enjoy the sermon?"

The pink spread throughout her face, and he knew then that she hadn't heard a word. Such a delight to him, this woman.

"Oh, yes," she said. "Did you?"

"I must admit I was a bit distracted," he said.

"Oh." Her eyes widened and darkened to the gray of a summer storm cloud.

With her as pink and flustered as she was, he decided to try his luck. "Would you like to take a walk with me this afternoon?"

She looked around, but her family had kindly disappeared.

"I should—" She pointed blindly to where Frank should have been. "I suppose I should ask Frank or my father, but they're not here."

"We can go find them if you like."

"No." She drew the syllable out as if arguing with herself. "I suppose I could go. But not for too long."

He smiled. A small victory, but the sweetest he'd ever won. "We won't be gone long. I promise."

~~~

The precision of the rows of potatoes stretching before Laura were soothing, a balm to the turmoil that had swirled within her during the walk over.

She and Marcus had spoken of only trivial things, each carefully avoiding the disastrous proposal of last week. Yet there was still a tingling awareness between them, a crackling in the air that made her skin prickle each time he brushed against her.

"You love this land, don't you?" she asked the man at her side.

She already knew the answer, could see it in the care that was evident in every row, in every plant, in the tidy care he took of his little house. Still, she wanted to hear the words and pretend they were about her.

"I do." Simple as a vow and as powerful as one.

"Did you send all those people to visit us this week?" she asked. "Mr. Harper, Mrs. Crivelli, all of them?"

She knew the answer to that too.

"I asked if they might want to look in on your folks," he admitted, "since they seemed lonely."

"They were. I couldn't see that, since I couldn't look past—" She sighed when the rest wouldn't come. "Thank you."

"I didn't do anything." He sounded as if he actually believed that.

"Yes, you did. You may think it was nothing, but it was everything." She paused, wondering if she should ask the rest. "Did you send all those young men too?"

"Young men?" His voice became the most delicious growl. "What young men?"

She worked hard to keep her mouth straight. His temper was delightful. Adorable. "Oh, Luke Crivelli and some others," she said as if it were of no consequence. "I thought you might have sent them since you felt sorry for me."

He muttered something she didn't catch, then said, "No, I didn't send them."

"I suppose they came on their own then." Just as airy as before and designed to tease him.

Marcus's jaw went tight, the line of it as sharp as a blade before softening again. "Do you know the first time I ever saw you?"

She shook her head, wondering where he was going with this.

"You were in the store, and you were waiting on Old Man Sweeney."

She remembered now. The old man lived high up in the mountains, eschewing all human contact until he needed supplies. Most people in Cabrillo avoided him, and he returned the favor.

"You were so kind with him," Marcus said with something close to wonder, "so patient."

"He was a customer." There was nothing unusual in how she'd treated him.

Marcus shook his head. "It was more than that. Most people would have turned him out. But you saw him as a person and treated him that way. Not too sweet, not too mean, but one person to another. I don't think anyone in this town had ever treated him that way."

"I remember he didn't seem to appreciate it much," she said wryly.

"No, but that didn't stop you." He looked out over the field. "I have something to tell you. To offer you."

She went still. What would she do if he proposed again? A few days of happiness with her parents hadn't changed the situation.

But oh, how she wanted to say yes. It was dangerous, this urge within her that grew stronger every day. If it grew strong enough, it would overpower her sense of duty.

And then she would lose all sense of herself.

He took a deep breath, the barrel of his chest growing even larger. "I know that you don't want to leave your parents," he rushed out.

She blinked. Had she ever directly said so to him? She couldn't remember it.

"And I know you're worried that I can't support four people," he went on.

The breath caught in her throat. He saw all that?

"You're right to be worried," he said. "I couldn't support all of us, especially with a bad harvest."

Her eyes began to sting. It was hopeless then.

"But if I sold this land and went back down to the valley to work on the family farm, I could do it," he finished.

Her heart stopped, and she swung her head up to stare at the fields before them.

He was going to give this up. For her. Not only for her, but for her parents as well.

They could be married.

A small speck of joy glittered within her at the thought before being consumed by dark practicality.

They would have to leave Cabrillo. Instead of being his own man, on his own land, he'd be another one of the countless Grieses.

She couldn't do that to him. She would have to say no again—this time not for her parents, but for him.

"Please." It was a whisper, but it was all she could manage with the magnitude of what he was willing to do for her. "Please, don't do that."

His head dropped. The defeated line of his shoulders wrenched at her, but she kept her hands firmly by her sides.

"I know how much this land means to you," she said, "how much being independent means. I couldn't ask you to give all that up. Not for me."

"It would be worth it. For you." So fervent. Enough belief there to almost sway her.

Almost.

"It might seem that way at first, but after a few years, you'd realize how much you'd given up, and we'd sink down into the same bitterness my parents are in. We'd choke on all that acrimony—yours and mine and my parents'."

He turned to her, and his face blazed with intensity, his brown eyes alight with determination.

It terrified her.

"Promise me you won't sell your land," she begged.

"I won't then. But I'm not finished. Even if it takes years, I'll wait for you. Until I have the money, or until you can leave your parents, I'll wait. You're all I want, ever since I saw you waiting on Sweeney in that store. I won't ask you to wait, but know this: I'll wait until the end of time for you. I swear it."

CHAPTER TEN

HE WOULD WAIT FOR HER.

This wonderful, kind man would wait. It seemed too good to be true. Whatever was it about her—plain, simple Laura Kemper—that would inspire him to such devotion?

His devotion, his ardor—his passion—nearly took her breath away.

"You don't have to do this." Pain stabbed at her as she said it, but she had to give him the chance to turn back. No man should wait years. Especially not a man such as Marcus, and not for a girl like her.

His eyes were alight with a fire that threatened to singe them both. "You don't understand. I *do* have to."

She swallowed hard and pressed her tongue to the seam of her lips, at last voicing the question gnawing at her. "But why?"

His smile was more of a grimace. "I only want to be with you. And if you won't be my wife, I'll have no other."

She raised a hand to his cheek, thinking to soothe away the tension in his jaw, his beard soft against her skin.

He breathed a kiss into her palm.

The warmth of his breath, his life, stealing across her skin melted the last of her defenses as if they were no more than spun sugar.

"Yes." It was as soft and yielding as his breath against her skin, but she meant it as fervently as he did. "I'll wait with you, and when the time is right, I will be your wife."

He breathed another kiss into her palm in response, never saying a word. She knew that he could not trust himself to speak just now, her sensitive, shy, adoring farmer.

A boldness snuck through her, made her daring. If he did love her, and they were to be married—eventually— was what she was about to suggest shocking?

"Would you kiss me again?" she ventured. "Properly?"

He groaned into her hand. "Sweetheart, if I touch you, I won't be able to stop."

She moved closer until their bodies were a breath apart. "Please?" She couldn't believe this was her, being called sweetheart and begging for a man's mouth on her own.

He loosed a ragged groan, then clasped her waist, his large hands almost meeting round it. His hands rested there for the space of two heartbeats, then slid up to just under her breasts before traveling down to the start of the swell of her hips. He repeated the caress a few times, never once passing the boundary he'd set for himself. Muted as it was by the layers between her skin and his hands, it wasn't nearly as satisfying as his mouth on hers had been.

He lowered his forehead to meet hers, his breathing as rough as his touch was controlled. "I can't do much more than this. I won't dishonor you." It was said as fiercely as his vow to wait for her.

"Then let's just keep doing this." She raised her hands to his shoulders, pulling him down for another one of those fevered kisses. The muscles beneath her hands were thick and taut as steel, a testament to the manual labor he performed. He could probably lift her as easily as he would a kitten, without even a thought. A shiver went through her at the image.

She slid her hands down, feeling the roughness of the linen against her palms and the hidden skin under it.

What did that skin feel like? She'd never seen a man's bare chest, much less touched one.

His tongue slid along her own. Perhaps his skin was as soft and as hot as his tongue.

She wanted to touch him. She wanted it more than her next breath.

As she slid her hands down his chest, the tension and heat of him radiated straight through the fabric to burn her palms. She ran the backs of her hands along the plane of his abdomen, noticing how it tightened as if the caress pained him. How intriguing.

His groan made her look up. His face was shuttered, his eyes half-closed, but the intensity remained. He might look as if he were in a dream state, but she sensed that every bit of his attention was focused on her and what she was about to do.

It made her head spin, to be so wholly the focus of his regard.

She ran her fingers over his torso again and again, his body jerking with each pass. Then, due to some devil she didn't even know was in her, she lowered her hand to the bulge below the waistband of his trousers, skimming her fingertips across it.

"Dear God," he muttered as he grabbed at her shoulders for support.

"Did it hurt?" She thought she might already know the answer, but since this was all so new to her, she wanted to be certain.

He shook his head.

A wicked smile curved her lips, one she'd never used before. It was quite nice, wearing that smile. "I'll just do it again then, shall I?"

This time his hips bucked against her, pressing a strange hardness into her hand. It wasn't so much the press of that hardness against her palm that was so fascinating—it was the expression on his face, eyes shuttered, brows drawn, lip caught between his teeth. All of her thrummed and tightened at the sight of his face. She rubbed again, and he made a strange kind of moan.

"Still doesn't hurt?" she asked. Perhaps she was taking this too far.

"You're killing me." He barely got it out through his gritted teeth. He caught her hands just as her fingers went for another touch.

"You can't... I can't..."

His eyes held hers, and she couldn't say if they were begging her to stop or go ahead. They stayed motionless together like that for a beat, her hands wanting to go farther while his imprisoned them.

"I can't handle much more." His voice was a rasp against her ears.

"Was I not supposed to do that?" She didn't know the rules to this game, not that she suspected he did either.

His throat bobbed as he rubbed a hand across his face. "No. Yes." He drew a shuddering breath. "I mean, you can, but not until we're married."

"Do you want me to do that when we're married?"

"Please God, yes."

"Language, Marcus," she chided. Then she laughed, dizzy with power and desire. And perhaps a touch drunk on the intensity of his response to her.

She could see why young girls were advised against allowing liberties to young men. Such a heady sensation was too potent to be put in the hands of foolish young ladies.

He caught her mouth again, this time with an urgency, a force that he didn't even try to contain. When he pulled away, she went to follow, but he kept her at arm's length.

"You can't... I can't...," he protested as his nose and ears went delightfully red.

She recognized that as his way of saying *enough* and folded her hands into her skirt.

He walked with a slight hitch to his step the whole way back.

~~~

The next week continued much the same as the last, with Mr. Harper and other residents of the town coming to call on the Kempers often. Laura greeted everyone with a smile but kept her and Marcus's secret to herself, cupping it to her heart for her own private enjoyment.

Marcus came to call every day, even if only for a few minutes to say hello and ask how she was. Neither of them mentioned marriage or even an engagement, but it seemed that everyone realized there was an understanding between them.

Rose and Frank let them alone when Marcus was at the mercantile, and perhaps Mrs. Kemper's glares at Marcus had softened, if only a bit. It was hard to tell what her father thought, but whether that was due to his illness or his actual ambivalence toward Marcus, she couldn't say.

Laura decided to stop worrying and simply enjoy the days. Spring was here, her family finally seemed content, and she had a young man who adored her. Worrying about the future could wait.

But when Catarina came for a visit one Saturday, she was not so sanguine.

"Are you and Marcus Gries engaged or not?" she demanded. She was unusually peevish, perhaps because her plan with the doctor had failed.

"Why do you ask?" Laura wouldn't let her friend's irritation ruffle her.

"Everyone in town says you are, but you're not wearing a ring. Not even Marcus would be so awful as to not get you a ring. And if you are engaged, why didn't you tell me?"

Laura sighed. She knew they'd be the cause of talk around town, but it was still unpleasant to be confronted with it. "No, we are not engaged."

Catarina let out a low, slow breath, sinking back into her chair in the parlor. "Well, I'm glad then."

Laura felt the bile rise within her. "Why? Are you jealous that I might be engaged and you're not?"

Her friend blinked in surprise. Even Laura was a bit shocked at what she'd said.

"I think you could do much better than Marcus," Catarina said.

Laura ground her back teeth together. "Better than Marcus? Better than a man who cares so deeply for me?"

Something rank and sharpish came into Catarina's face. "I beg your pardon. Has Marcus come into some money from a rich, dead relation? Because just last week you were in this very room, sobbing over him, and now it seems he can do no wrong."

Laura fisted her hands and rose to her feet. "I never knew you thought me so mercenary. But no, he has no inheritance."

"Well then, you can't marry him, now can you?" Catarina raised her chin pugnaciously.

"Says who?"

"You said yourself it was no matter if he was looking for a wife, he wouldn't find one in you," Catarina said. "And now I hear you two are thick as thieves."

The accusation in Catarina's tone was like sandpaper against Laura's nerves.

"Perhaps he simply enjoys my company. Is that so difficult to believe?"

Catarina puffed with disdain. "You must have done something to entice him. And if you did, you must mean to marry him. That makes you a liar."

Rage flamed under Laura's skin. "Not every girl in this town is as marriage mad as you are," she spit out.

"Not every girl has to throw herself at any passing man's head. Although, a fat lot of good that's done you so far."

When Catarina blanched white as bone, Laura knew she had gone too far.

They both had gone too far.

"Cat, I—"

But Laura's apology died in her throat as the other girl's expression twisted into one of beseeching sorrow.

Catarina raised her hands in supplication. "Laura, what are we doing? What has taken hold of us?"

Laura felt the anger drain from her, and her hands relaxed against her skirts as she sank back into the chair, shaken by their spat. "I... I don't know." It was foul, whatever it was. "I'm afraid I wasn't entirely honest just now. Marcus and I are not engaged, but we do have an... an agreement."

Catarina deserved to know, and Laura regretted not telling her sooner. The pleasure of keeping that secret for herself was now entirely gone.

Catarina's eyes screwed up as she tried to translate that. "An agreement? But what of your parents?"

"He said he would wait."

"Years even?"

Laura gave a small nod, pleasure shimmering through her as she remembered their last walk when he had promised everything.

Catarina's beautiful face softened and grew wistful. "Then I suppose he is worthy of you."

Laura sighed, feeling tears prickling in her throat. To have Catarina say that, given how she felt about Marcus—it was a beautifully generous concession.

But then Catarina burst into tears.

Now it was Laura's turn to make soothing noises and pat her friend's hand. "What's wrong?" But she suspected she already knew the answer.

"I am happy for you, really I am," her friend said through great gulps of tears, "and I only wanted you to be happy, and I knew you would have to marry a man who could support you and your parents—"

Laura kept patting and nodding.

"—that was why I suggested the doctor. I knew Marcus didn't have the income to marry you. But if you truly want to wait for him, well, then, I am happy for you."

"Forgive me," Laura said gently, "but you don't sound happy."

Catarina rubbed at her eyes. "I know it's unworthy of me. You've been such a friend to me, but—" She took a shuddering breath. "But I am jealous."

How hard that must have been for Catarina to admit. And hard for Laura to hear, that her happiness was the cause of her friend's suffering.

Laura rose, gathered up Catarina in an embrace. "It will be your turn next," she said. "And don't feel badly.

This marriage business will drive all of us mad in the end, I'm certain."

It had certainly driven the two of them mad for several moments this afternoon.

Catarina fished a handkerchief from her skirt pocket and dabbed at her eyes. "I fear that it will never be my turn. I'm already twenty-five. I've been trying for so long." She looked off into the distance, as if seeing her future as a spinster there. Then she gave a full-bodied shake and, with a tangible effort, tossed away her sad expression. "But let's discuss this agreement that is not an engagement. I am curious. If he fancied you, why did it take him so long to start courting you?"

"To be honest, I think he was afraid of you. We're almost always together at dances and socials and such."

"Pfft. How could he be afraid of me?"

Laura had to laugh. "Catarina, sometimes you look as if you could eat up every man in this town before supper and clean your teeth with their bones."

Catarina's shoulders shook as she began giggling uncontrollably. Laura helplessly joined in as well, the two girls laughing until they were breathless.

After a bit, her friend sobered. "You really do care for him, don't you?"

"I do. Very much." The first time she'd admitted it aloud—it was liberating to finally put her feelings to words. She ought to do it more often.

Her friend squeezed her hand. "I pray he'll make you as happy as I know you'll make him." Catarina's mouth twisted ruefully. "That is, whenever you two actually become betrothed."

A cold shimmer of unease ran through Laura. She'd told herself to simply enjoy the days as they came, but it had only been a week of waiting. Would she be so carefree after a year? Or two?

And what of Marcus? It was well and good to claim he would wait forever in the heat of the moment, but that heat would dissipate with time. It would have to.

She shoved those thoughts down deep, to the depths of her mind where she could not see them.

She would do well to remember not to worry on a future that had not yet arrived.

CHAPTER ELEVEN

MARCUS WASN'T SURE HOW MUCH more he could take.

When he told her she could touch him and he wouldn't touch her, he hadn't realized she'd use it to drive him slowly insane.

Every spare moment they had away from prying eyes, she'd taken the opportunity to touch or taste a little more of him. A kiss breathed into his neck, a hand brushed against his thigh, or dear God, even higher...

Like a laudanum fiend, he'd kept coming back for more.

Before all this, he'd considered himself a normal sort of man, tending to *that need* once a day, usually in the morning when he first awoke. Now that Laura teased him every chance she got, he was having to tend to himself morning, noon, and night.

He'd have to marry her soon if he wanted to get any work on the farm done.

It was Sunday again, and he'd have hours alone with her out in the fresh spring air. His hands shook as he buttoned his shirt, remembering how she had run her hands down his chest only a week before.

Surviving through the church service was looking less and less likely.

But when he saw her sitting in the pew, her hair a golden halo framing that beautiful face, he was mesmerized, unable to do anything except slide in beside her, knowing he'd suffer the torments of the damned with her leg pressed against his throughout the service.

It was like getting a taste of the delights of heaven while being prodded with the pitchfork of Old Scratch.

Fortunately, he was able to stand at the end without embarrassment and escort her back to the mercantile for Sunday dinner. He breathed a sigh of relief once they were finally out of doors and headed to the creek.

She smiled up at him. "They are a bit wearying."

"Your parents?" He'd been thinking of something else entirely. "No, they're fine. I just like having you all to myself for a little bit."

Her eyes went smoky. "Oh, do you?"

He wanted to groan and laugh all at the same time. This woman was going to kill him. And it would be delicious.

He quickened his step. "Let's get to the creek."

She laughed knowingly but kept right up.

They settled near the shade of a pine tree, its unchanging needles a stark contrast to the unfurling new growth on every other tree as spring brought them back to life. The creek gurgled playfully alongside them, freed from its winter cage of ice.

He plucked some penstemon, carefully threading them through her hair, admiring the purple-blue of the blooms against the golden strands.

"You look"—he reached for the right words, wishing he knew more poetry—"like a woodland fairy."

She smiled—that warm, lovely smile that had stolen his heart the first time he'd ever seen it. "I'd make a pretty poor fairy. No wings, no magic—just plain, simple me."

He tucked a bloom in more securely, enjoying the silken caress of her hair. If only he could trust himself to touch the rest of her. "I'm glad you're real. I couldn't grab hold of a fairy."

She smiled that teasing smile, the one he loved almost as much as the smile he'd first fallen in love with. "But you won't grab hold of me, will you? Not until we're married."

"I can't. Once I touch you, I don't trust myself not to go too far. And I won't dishonor you like that."

"But I can still touch you." Her hands went to his chest, rubbing with obvious pleasure.

She traced the lines of his chest for a time, her hands spreading fire throughout him in their wake.

Her gaze caught his and held. And then slowly her hands traveled to the buttons of his shirt.

Her eyes held a question. A request. A demand.

He ought to stop her—her touch on his bare skin was a torture too far—but he found his voice no longer worked.

She eased the first four buttons free, paused with the placket of his shirt gripped in her hands while he forgot to breathe.

Before he remembered how his lungs worked, her hands were on his skin, tangling with the short hair on his chest.

His blood thickened with desire, his heart thrumming in time with the ache developing in his groin. He should stop her, should capture those clever, teasing hands before he went completely mad, but he knew he wouldn't. If these were the crumbs he had to settle for until they married, he'd take them, by God.

Her face was a portrait in passionate intensity. Those smoky eyes were half-lidded, fixed on her hands as she traced them over his skin, catching at the peaks of his nipples with each pass and sending lightning stabbing through him with each tug.

This endless fascination with his body was a puzzle of hers that he had yet to piece together. She was the beautiful one, the one who should be painted and praised, a goddess come to Earth. Whereas he was only a mortal, and a farmer at that.

But he didn't dare voice his misgivings, especially when her curiosity was so satisfying to them both. One day he'd satisfy his own curiosity about her. Hopefully one day soon.

Finished with his chest, her hands moved lower, hesitating at the waist of his trousers. He ought to grab those tormenting little hands, ought to tell her no, but he couldn't. He was discovering that the only thing he could deny her was... nothing.

So instead he held still, granting her permission with his silence, tensing every muscle in his body, steeling himself for what would be the worst—and best—part of the whole ordeal.

She didn't undo the buttons there, for which he was profoundly grateful, just rubbed her hand along the bulge between his legs.

Just. As if the motion of her fingers weren't echoing throughout his entire body.

He struggled to pull air into his lungs, his heart banging against his rib cage. His body shuddered with the slow strokes of her fingers, his mind filled with images of her lying beneath him, his length stroking her in her most intimate spot in that exact rhythm.

After an eternity of it, he could take no more. He set his hands on her shoulders and gently put space between them. But she clutched at his arms and sank to the ground, pulling him over her and raising her lips to his.

He devoured the mouth that had tormented him as she offered it up. His hips bucked against the cradle of her pelvis, finding only harsh cloth instead of the softness he knew lay beneath.

He pulled her skirts up to her waist, growling against her mouth when again he encountered only cloth at the junction of her legs. He moved lower to rub his mouth against the unprotected skin of her neck.

It was the soft noise she made that brought him back to himself. A mewl of either pleasure or pain—he couldn't tell which—but one he'd never heard from her before.

He shoved himself back and stared in horror at the scene before him. Laura, sprawled in the grass, her hair wild and free, her face and neck raw from his mouth, and her skirts hiked up to her waist, her long legs in their white pantaloons exposed to the world.

He'd dreamed of making love to her like this, with her hair loose and nothing but the sky for cover, but this—this was a nightmare.

"I'm so sorry," he ground out. The words were weak against the reality before him. "I never meant for this to happen."

She simply stared at him, her chest rising and falling with the effort of her breathing.

He ran a hand through his hair, tugging hard in an attempt to bring himself back to reason.

"I don't think I can do this anymore." He hadn't intended to say that, but it was true. Hadn't he just proven that he couldn't do this? At least not with his honor intact. The erection jutting against his pants proved it beyond a doubt.

She slowly came up to her elbows, her face now white under the burn left by his mouth.

"You can't do this?" The shock in her voice cut at him. Lord, how badly had he scared her just now?

"No." He shook his head, then buttoned himself back up with shaking hands. "I'm only a man. It's too much."

She watched him silently, her face wary.

"I suppose you had better take me home then." Her whisper was tinged with something bitter. He might have said it sounded like defeat, but she'd lost no battle, not as he had. It must have been disappointment. Disappointment in him and his base animal urges.

She shook her skirts down and tied her bonnet around her gloriously tousled hair. Her family was sure to know what they'd been up to when she walked in like that, but he supposed there was no help for it now.

He held out his arm for her, but she angrily jerked away. She couldn't even bear to touch him anymore, it seemed. Head hanging, he took the hint and trudged behind, letting her set the pace.

~~~

Laura strode angrily away, uncaring if he followed her. Humiliation and rage and uncertainty burned at her. What a fool she had been, thinking there would be happiness for her. It had only been a few weeks, and already he had turned her away. And after the wanton things she had done with him...

"You said you would wait!" Her angry shout sent a burst of quail out from the brush, their wings flapping wildly as they broke for someplace safe, far from her raised voice.

He looked nearly as startled as the quail. "I did wait," he shouted back.

"What, a few weeks? You said you'd wait for years if necessary."

He frowned, looking angry and puzzled at once. "I waited just now. I didn't take advantage of you."

"Didn't you? First you said that you'd wait, and now you say that you can't do this anymore."

"Well, I can't! You can only tease a man so much before he loses his mind."

"A tease? I'm a tease?" She recalled those terrible words she had thrown at Catarina during their quarrel, and shame grabbed at her throat. "You're the one who teased me by making me hope for better things. I was perfectly happy before."

"No, you weren't. I could see you weren't. I thought I might be able to make you happy, but—" He shook his head, all befuddled male impotence.

"But you're weak," she finished for him.

"Laura, do you know how terrible it is to have you touch me all over and never be able to touch you back? I think about it constantly, even in my dreams. The farm's going to the devil because I can't think straight. I can't do this. It's... too much."

I can't do this. It's too much. Each word was a splinter embedded in her heart.

It was over. And so soon.

It was exactly what she'd feared. That he'd realize that she was nothing special, nothing worth waiting years for.

And it was a thousand times worse than she'd imagined.

"You said you would wait." Her voice trembled along with her chin. "You said you would wait forever if that's what it took. But you lied."

She ran past him and away, not turning once. Even as he called for her, over and over and over again.

CHAPTER TWELVE

ROSE WAS STILL SETTING THE kitchen to rights when Laura burst in.

Her face was aflame and her lungs heaved from her long run back to the mercantile, but now finally she'd reached safety. She could stop running.

She hung onto the doorway, needing help to stay upright. If she let go, she might sink to the floor and howl.

"Laura!" Her mother's shocked tone had Rose looking up from the sink. "Whatever have you been up to! I declare, your father and I didn't raise you to—"

"What happened?" Rose's words to her were more command than question.

Laura licked her lips, which were dry from her wild flight, and attempted to draw air to answer. "We're not—" Not what, engaged any longer? Technically, they never had been. "Marcus and I—" She closed her eyes as the pain of what had just happened finally caught her.

"Why are you two speaking English?" her mother whined in Dutch.

Frank, sitting at the table with their mother, took that moment join in as well. "Laura, what has gotten into you?" His face fell as he looked her over. "Don't tell me you had another fight—"

"Everyone out!" Rose yelled in English. "Frank, take your mother. Laura and I need to talk."

Her brother complied instantly, taking their mother by the arm and, as gently as he could, leading her out of the room even as she protested. Laura could only watch as Rose forced her will in a manner Laura had never thought her capable of.

"Now," Rose said, wiping her hands on a rag and turning to face Laura full-on, "you and I are going to speak about this young man, your parents, and your future."

Laura sat herself down at the table, breath still sawing, never looking away from Rose. Or more accurately, at the stranger who seemed to have taken hold of Rose.

Her sister-in-law sat across from her with a sigh. "Tell me what happened between you and Marcus this afternoon. You two were so happy together these few weeks—yes, we all noticed—and now you're a storm of weeping again."

Laura pinched the fingertips of her left hand between the thumb and forefinger of her right, squeezing each finger in turn before beginning all over again. "Marcus promised me that he would wait as long as necessary to marry me, but today he... he said that he could wait no longer. So." She shrugged, her shoulders aching with the effort.

Rose's face went white as guilt stole over her features. "He was waiting because you promised me you wouldn't leave, wasn't he?"

Laura looked back to her fingers and directed her nod to them.

"I'm afraid," Rose said in a choked voice. "I'm afraid I have been unfair to you."

Laura looked up at that, shock making her face slacken. "No, you've been more than fair, taking care of my parents, bearing the brunt of—"

Her sister-in-law waved that off. "I wanted you here for my own selfish reasons—and to ease my burdens. I remembered something these past weeks, as we all in this family reawakened to joy. Something I learned when Frank and I first fell in love, something I had forgotten that I should not have."

Leaning in, Laura wondered what Rose could possibly be referring to.

"I remembered this week that love does not come cheaply," Rose continued, "at least not love that is true, love that is enduring. We all pay a price, and your mother is the price I pay for loving Frank."

Laura pondered that for a moment before protesting, "But Mother shouldn't be your price to pay. She's my mother! My duty."

Rose shook her head. "The problem is you're too much like your mother."

Laura could feel the sparks flashing from her eyes and she opened her mouth to protest.

Her sister-in-law held up a hand. "Hear me out. When your father first fell ill and didn't want to go out anymore, what was your mother's reaction?"

"To always stay with him."

"And when they decided to entomb themselves in these back rooms, what was your reaction?"

Laura's mouth tightened. "That was different." Her mother's reaction had nothing to do with hers.

"Truly? Then why did you say no to the proposal of a fine man who loves you?"

"It was duty." She nearly hissed the words.

"Exactly what your mother would say." Rose reached across the table and seized Laura's hands. "Don't let *duty* kill your chance. And the price you will pay for your love is to know that you left me here with your mother."

Laura blinked at the tears gathering in her eyes, feeling as if the emotions swirling within her were attacking her from the inside.

Was Rose correct? Was there always a price to pay for true love?

Soft footfalls came down the hallway before Frank appeared in the doorway. "Laura, there's someone here to see you."

Her stomach lurched. There was only one person it could be, and the reckoning he brought with him terrified her.

Marcus appeared behind Frank, his face as blank as a new sheet of paper. It seemed the events of this afternoon had touched him not at all.

Rose pushed her chair back. "Frank, I believe these two have matters to discuss."

Then Rose and Frank were gone and she and Marcus were alone. He crossed the room toward her, and as he did, she turned her face from him, unable to bear the thought of looking at him when she was so raw and he so calm.

He pulled one of her hands from the table and breathed a kiss across it. She turned to see what he was about, and to her astonishment, he was on his knees before her. Those beautiful brown eyes of his smiled up at her.

"You run quite fast," he said.

She could only blink in response. Where was his anger from earlier?

"Could you tell me what you thought I said today?" His voice was soft, amused, and so far from angry she might have dreamed their quarrel.

She swallowed hard at the memory. "You said you couldn't wait anymore. That you didn't want to marry me."

He shook his head, his lips brushing ever so slightly against her hand. "I never said I didn't want to marry you. I said I couldn't let you touch me anymore. Because I was going mad."

His lips against her skin were clouding her mind. "No, you didn't."

"I'm fairly certain I did." Another soft kiss, now pressed into her palm. "I think we may have had our first misunderstanding."

"Misunderstanding?"

He smiled up at her, a smile of such tenderness her heart squeezed. "When I kiss your hand, how do you feel?"

She only shook her head, confused by this. He kissed the pulse at her wrist, making her toes curl in her boots.

"How does that feel?"

All she could give in response was a shaky breath.

He then traced that same pulse with his tongue, and her entire body shivered with it.

She snatched her hand back before he set her aflame. "Marcus, I—" She dropped her hand as realization dawned on her. "Dear Lord, I've simply been tormenting you these weeks, haven't I?"

The poor man. And he'd never breathed a word to her or tried to stop her.

His smile tipped into naughtiness. "You can torment me all you like. But I think it's best to wait for that until after we're married, as the events of this afternoon proved."

She licked her lips. "You still wish to marry me?"

His face turned solemn, chasing the smile away. "I swore to wait, and I'll hold to that."

She looked at that beloved face of his, the gentle brown of his eyes, the sweetness of his mouth, and thought on the price she would have to pay to awaken to that face for the rest of her days. Was she ready to pay it, knowing that Rose was paying as well?

"I have something I need to ask you," she said, "but before I ask you that, I need to ask something else."

He cocked his head. "Go ahead. With the something else that comes before the something."

"If we were married, could my parents stay with us for part of the year? I know it would be hard, and if we hadn't the money, we couldn't do it, but if we did, could they stay? As a way to take some of the burden off Rose and Frank?" An inelegant heap of words, but it was the best she could manage.

He rubbed his thumb across her knuckles. "That would be fine with me. I don't mind your folks; they're not half as bad as you seem to think they are."

He said that now, but he might not be so confident after several months with her mother.

"It wouldn't be all the time," she said. "Perhaps a few weeks or months out of the year. But I'll still have to run into town to help them—"

He held up a hand. "Laura, it's perfectly fine with me. I would never expect you to abandon your family once we're married. Besides, we won't be moving to Timbuktu. You'd just be down the road and still able to take your mother to the Women's Temperance League meetings." Comprehension lightened his expression. "Wait, I thought we wouldn't be married until your parents passed. But you..."

She took a deep breath, finally ready to pay her price. "That was my other question. Marcus Gries, will you marry me?"

His hands tightened on hers, his throat working. "I already said I would. Whenever you're ready."

"No, I meant now. Well, perhaps not right now, but as soon as we can."

His eyes closed, and he simply breathed another kiss into her palm in answer. Truth be told, her own throat was too tight to speak.

"If that's what you want." He pushed the words out. "I'll do anything you want."

She gave him a sharp look. "Don't sell the farm. I definitely do not want that. Promise me you won't speak of it again."

"I won't. I swear."

Finally she felt as if she could smile again, so she did. "I suppose now that I have you at my mercy, I could get you to agree to anything."

"Anything?"

"Yes, like if I made you promise to kiss me— properly—every day of our married life."

He swallowed. "I think I could agree to that."

"But not before the wedding," she assured him. "I won't ask you to compromise your honor like that."

His answering smile was rueful. "Let's see if we can find the pastor at home today then."

She laughed softly. What a wonderful man she was marrying. "I want one last promise from you since you're still at my mercy."

"Anything." And she knew he meant it with all his heart.

"Promise me you'll spend the rest of our lives loving me as much as I love you?"

"Only if you promise me the same."

The happiness that lit within her was stronger than the spring sunlight. "I swear."

EPILOGUE

IT WAS A LOVELY WEDDING and the entire town wished them well.

Marcus thought that even if he lived for a century, he would never see anything as lovely as Laura coming down the church aisle, ready to become his wife, wearing the same dove-gray dress as when they'd first danced.

They had walked back to the farm after the wedding dinner at the Whitmans' barn, the rooms of the mercantile being too small for the entirety of the Gries family. Laura had waved off the buggy he'd borrowed, saying that walking had served them well in their courtship and would serve them well in their marriage.

Now they were on the porch—their front porch—hand in hand, looking at the door. He bent and swept her up, her breathy laugh as he did so softer than the kiss of a spring breeze. Holding his love in his arms, crossing the threshold of the home he would share with her, he felt greater than any knight in a story.

She smiled at him, a smile of such wondrous, expansive love and pride that he nearly stumbled. How would he ever be equal to the emotions shining through those smoke-blue eyes?

He wouldn't.

All he could do was love her with all his heart, as best he could, day after day, and hope that all the days of his life would sum up to something near to what was in her eyes.

Beginning today.

He gently set her down, enjoying the slide of her against him. She'd held off tormenting him in the weeks before the wedding but had taken to giving him long, slow, knowing looks when she could, looks that had set his blood aflame.

Tonight there would be more than looks. Much, much more.

The house smelt of spring and sawdust, the spring coming in with the sunlight through the open windows, the sawdust from the addition he was building to house her parents. But that didn't concern him now. Her scent, soft and light, yet more potent than the blooms of spring, was what did concern him. That, and how he was going to accomplish what was next expected of him.

The thought of finally having her, completely and to-tally, as he'd dreamed of, made him tremble. He wanted it to be perfection for her since she deserved only that, but he had no idea of how to achieve it. Oh, he knew the general mechanics of what went where, but he had yet to test the practicalities. He would simply have to trust her to lead him when it came to her pleasure.

He threaded his fingers through hers as they walked to the bedroom. He waited, letting her take in the room for the very first time. She'd sent over some quilts and bed linens earlier in the week, and he'd made up the bed with them, wanting her to feel at home and at ease. He must have done something right, because a pleased smile lit her face.

And then she was tugging at his hand, leading them to the bed. He gingerly sat on the edge next to her, unsure of what to do next. Kiss her? Undress her? Talk to her?

She bit at her lower lip as she nervously glanced at him before putting on a too-wide smile. "So," she said slowly, making it almost a question.

"Yes?"

She blinked at him for a moment, then a true smile came to her lips. "Are you as nervous as I am?" she whispered.

With those words, his nerve steadied. She was depending on him, would depend on him for the rest of her days. He could do this for her. He could do anything, for her.

He lifted their entwined hands and kissed her knuckles, enjoying the satin of her skin. "Tell me what you want to do."

A rosy pink stole over her face, and she shook her head at him. "I can't say, I can only..." She lifted her hand to his shirt, trying to unbutton it.

He closed his hand over hers. "No. Tell me what you want me to do to *you.*"

If she was pink before, she was definitely red now. Her mouth opened, but nothing emerged.

He kissed the inside of her wrist, savoring the heat of her pulse under the skin. "Laura," he whispered against it, "tell me what you want. Trust me."

Her eyes fluttered closed, as gently as leaves shimmering in a spring breeze. "I want... will you... would you... touch me?" The last two words were the faintest whisper, but still he heard them.

"You'll need to help me with your clothes," he said. "I'm afraid I don't know much about ladies' fastenings."

Her eyes opened at that, darkened now to nearly navy, and she lifted her hands to her dress. His own hands reached up to join hers, and together they unpeeled her many layers, between sweet, soft kisses.

Finally she stood before him, completely bare. As she raised her gaze to his, she thrust her chin out, a bit too fiercely, trying to be brave. He smiled at the gesture. She had no cause to be ashamed, not as perfectly made as she was.

Although he had never seen a lady fully unclothed before, he could not imagine any woman looking more divine than she did right now. From the top of her golden head to the tips of her pink toes, every curve, every line, set his groin to throbbing, especially the curves and lines between her shoulders and her thighs. He looked over her greedily, lingering on the secret places he wanted to explore with his hands and mouth. Something in his expression must have reassured her because her face slowly relaxed, and a small smile even began to tease at her mouth.

"Do you think you might also undress? I'm feeling a bit..." She gestured to her unclothed form.

He stripped off his clothes faster than he'd ever thought possible, only slightly embarrassed when his erection sprang free from his underclothes. But if she could stand before him like that, he could do it as well.

He caught up her hand again, needing the anchor of her touch in this new and unusual realm of being nude with another person. "Tell me what you want," he asked again, burning with the need to touch her but wanting her permission, her direction.

She leaned in close, kissing him as she laid his hand on her breast. His breath slipped from his lungs as he finally felt her softness beneath his palm. His fingers found the peak of her nipple and gently explored, making her whimper against his mouth.

His hand stilled as he whispered against her lips, "Did I hurt you? You have to tell me if it hurts." Drat his callused hands. They were too rough for her delicate skin.

"No," she whispered back. "It feels... good. Too good."

He smiled, then returned to kissing and caressing her, raising his hand to capture her other breast, lavishing them both with strokes and squeezes until she was panting against his mouth and rubbing her lower half against his. His erection throbbed dangerously at the brush of her heated curls, but he concentrated on ignoring the sensation. There would be time enough for that when she asked him to.

"What else do you want me to do?"

She looked at him with pleasure-bleared eyes and seemed to be trying to remember how to speak. "I want you to touch—" She stopped and buried her head in his shoulder, her breath hot against his chest. "I can't say. I simply can't say it."

He decided to be daring. He ran his hand down her torso until he came to the soft curls that tormented him so, then reached lower, to the damp, secret place between her legs.

"Here?" he said roughly, the heat from her core flooding into him and melting his control.

She nodded frantically against his shoulder, a strange kind of moan coming from her as he moved his hand against her. He hesitated for a moment, wondering if he had gone too far. Then, wonder of wonders, she pressed that secret place hard against his hand, and he knew he'd done the right thing. He explored her with his fingers, loving the soft slickness there, trying to imagine how it might look in the spring sunlight with Laura all undone upon their bed and her legs spread wide to welcome him.

His arousal became a thrum in his blood until he could no longer hear her soft whimpers above it. When she lifted her head from his shoulder and kissed him more fiercely than she ever had before, he knew it was time.

Lifting her as gently as he could, he set her down on the bed, arranging her just as he'd fantasized. But the reality before him was finer than any imaginings.

She looked at him with heavy eyes, her limbs supple, the secret place between her legs flushed rose pink with her pleasure. He lowered himself down to her, pausing briefly to kiss her before positioning himself at her center. Then he began to move forward, inch by slow inch, watching her as he did so, looking for any sign of distress on her face.

When he was halfway home, she shut her eyes tightly.

He swallowed hard and halted. "Does it hurt?"

She shook her head but kept her eyes shut tight. "It's... I don't know how to describe it."

"Do you want me to stop?" He might die on the spot, but he would do it.

Her eyes opened then. "No. I want you to go deeper."

So he did. Once he was fully within her, he finally allowed himself to simply feel what it was like to have her completely surrounding him.

No one had ever said it could be like this, that he would see stars even with his eyes fully open. He began to move within her, the slip and pull against his member the most exquisite sensation he had ever experienced.

She began to move with him, hesitantly at first, before catching the rhythm of it and sending him beyond what he could have even dreamed possible. They moved together, straining toward one another, until he felt a wave of something indescribable build to the most terrific peak.

His seed came forth from him, planting within her as surely as life planted itself within the soil outside, taking root and flourishing as his love for her was now, spreading throughout him and flowing out, as he said again and again, "I love you, I love you, I love you."

She arched to meet him one last time, then pulled him close with her entire self. As he lay against her, both of them damp with passion and the afterpulses of his pleasure still wracking him, she pressed soft, lingering kisses against his cheek and neck.

"I love you too," she breathed against him, and his heart filled to overflowing at the words dancing across his skin.

"Am I hurting you?" he mumbled into the pillow. He levered himself off her with a huge effort. "Did I hurt you?"

Her answering smile nearly blinded him with its radiance, stronger than the sun at noon. "No, it was... perfect."

~~~

Laura sat wrapped in a robe on the front porch, enjoying the sunset from her very own rocker, set next to Marcus's. Her body twitched and twinged in the most delicious places, reminding her of what they had just done. She didn't think she could love Marcus any more, but the worshipful way he had loved her had proved her wrong.

The man himself came out to the porch then, carrying two cups of lemonade and humming a little tune. He handed one cup to her, kissing her as he did, then sat next to her in his rocker, reaching across the distance to take her hand.

They had rocked together like that in companionable silence, enjoying the sunset for several moments before she realized what he had been humming.

And then she had to laugh. "The Farmer in the Dell." He'd been humming a song about a farmer taking a wife.

He squeezed her hand. "What's so amusing?"

She smiled into the sunset. "I'll tell you later. Let's enjoy this sunset while it lasts."

She knew that they had a lifetime of sunsets and laughter to look forward to.

ACKNOWLEDGEMENTS

As usual, the biggest thanks go to my critique partner, Emma Barry. And thanks to the team at Victory Editing for making the book shine.

Thanks also go to Melody and Cindy, world's greatest lab mates, who still know what they did. For career and self publishing advice, the community at Romance Divas always comes through.

And of course, thank you to my family. For everything.

ABOUT THE AUTHOR

Genevieve Turner writes historical romance fresh from the Golden State. In a previous life, she was a scientist studying the genetics of behavior, but now she's a stay at home mom studying the intersection of nature and nurture in her own kids. (So far, nature is winning!) She lives in beautiful Southern California, where she manages her family and homestead in an indolent manner.

You can find her on the web at www.genturner.com.

34174374R00101

Made in the USA
Middletown, DE
10 August 2016